please,

please,

please

look for more books about

THE FRIENDSHIP RING:

if you only knew (Zoe's story)

not that i care (Morgan's story)

THE FRIENDSHIP RING

Rachel Vail

please,

please,

please

SCHOLASTIC INC.
NEW YORK TORONTO LONDON
AUCKLAND SYDNEY

ISBN 0-590-37452-4

Book design by David Saylor
The text type was set in 12-point Dante Medium.

12 11 10 9 8 7 6 5 8 9/9 0 1 2 3/0

Printed in the U.S.A. 40
First edition, July 1998

to

my

grandfather,

Harry Silverman,

with

love.

please,

please,

please

one

My mother has a very complex relationship with cows. Also with me. She grew up on a dairy farm, doing thick-booted chores in poop and milk drippings before dawn, fantasizing, while she mucked, of escaping to dance like a swan in the spotlight at Lincoln Center. Three days after her seventeenth birthday, instead of buying a dozen eggs and a jar of apple butter, she kept walking and used her grocery money plus what she'd hoarded over the years for a bus ticket. She never got onto the stage at Lincoln Center, but she did wait tables across the street for a few years, taking ballet classes and watching performances from the back with standing room tickets scraped from her tips. One night, the man standing beside her asked if she'd like a cup of coffee after. They got married, moved here, decorated the kitchen with a cow theme, and had me who might someday dance in the spotlight at Lincoln Center.

The only cows I know are pot holders and ceramic spoon handles. Milk comes from a carton, and I'm allergic to it. But every morning, my mother wakes me up before dawn to do my stretching, and although I don't fantasize about standing in poop instead, my mind does wander.

My mother is very proud of me.

I'm just like her.

two

I started ballet six years ago, and from the first day of class, I was obsessed. Outside of the ballet studio, I was just a gawky, frizz-headed, stuttering first grader; once class started, the work was hard but clear — straighter, longer, higher, slower. Grace. Ballet made sense to me like nothing else in the muddled, rushed world. I just knew how to do it. My brother, Paul, was two and already talking, so smart and cute like he still is, like Mom, so different from me. Dance class meant no words for an hour, relief. I was nuts for it — I listened only to ballet music and practiced until my legs shook. *Ballerina,* I used to say to myself, falling asleep. *Ballerina.*

But now I'm in seventh grade — maybe my favorite musician shouldn't be Tchaikovsky anymore. Maybe I should be eating cookies, even slouching occasionally, or crossing my legs (which I never do — it works against turn-out) — enough adagios, I think sometimes; I should be trudging with my friends though the mall on a Saturday, eating Gummi Bears, wearing a Boggs Bobcats soccer jersey with number five on the back. But then I lift myself up onto the tips of my toes and imagine waiting in the wings for my entrance. It's hard to know which I want more.

I came up here to my room after dinner tonight to try to figure it out. I told Mom and Dad and Paul I couldn't play catch with them because I had to work on my project for school tomorrow, but instead I'd stopped thinking and was just forcing my turn-out up on *pointe,* pressing the backs of my knees toward each other, listening to the beautiful *clock-clock* sound my brand-new toe shoes made *tap-tapping* against my wood floor.

My door opened and almost slammed me in the face. Mom.

"Ooo!" she said, at the same time as I said the same exact thing. "Phew," she breathed, her hand up near her long, graceful neck, like whenever she's nervous or startled. "So? How's it going?"

"Good," I said. "Fine." I stood in fifth position flat on the floor. Mom smiled down toward my feet, at the toe shoes I wasn't supposed to be trying on before getting my teacher's OK. "I just, I . . ."

"I always did that, too," Mom said. "How do they feel?"

“Perfect,” I said. We had just bought them a few hours earlier, and I couldn’t take my eyes off the cool pink satin.

She smiled. “Great. They look so beautiful.” She stood behind me, her fingertips gentle on my waist, and we looked at me in the mirror — my new pink leg warmers over pale pink tights, my new skinny-strap leotard, maroon, because now I’m in performance level. “I’m so proud of you,” Mom said. “Level Three.”

I balanced my head light on my shoulders, eyes steady and front. Not everyone gets invited up to Level Three.

“It really shows all the work you’ve been putting in is paying off.”

“Maybe,” I said, letting myself smile for a second. “I can’t do soccer, though.”

“I know,” Mom said. “That’ll be hard, huh?”

"Yeah," I said, lowering myself down to flat feet. "Not, not that I'm any good at soccer, but . . ."

"But any time you go against the crowd, it's hard," Mom agreed.

"Mmm." I rolled my head around to loosen up my neck.

"Well, when you get to be a Polichinelle this winter, and when your career blossoms like Darci Kistler's did . . ."

"If," I corrected, looking at the poster of Darci Kistler on my wall, daring to wonder for a second if I could ever have a career like hers. If I could, would it be worth giving up stomping around with my friends in the mud after school and taking the late bus home? Five dance classes a week is so much. Four days a week. It really means I can't do anything else.

Mom kissed my hair. "I have every confidence in you." She went over and sat down on my bed, her posture, as always, perfect but relaxed. I sat on the floor and pulled off my toe shoes, nestled them carefully inside each other, and slipped them into their white mesh bag. My mother looks like a young Jessica Lange — soft curls, soft features, soft eyes; casual but glamorous at the same time. I don't look like any movie stars. I look like my dad — deep-set eyes and a little blotchy.

As she straightened my pillows, Mom asked, "So? What are you putting in besides your toe shoes?"

My project for school, which I was supposedly working on, is to choose ten things that represent who I am and put them in the paper bag Mrs. Shepard, my English/social studies teacher, gave out Friday. Bring Yourself in a Sack, Mrs. Shepard called it. Of course the first thing I thought of was my new toe shoes. I hadn't gotten much beyond that with fifteen hours left before school tomorrow. There was a lot else on my mind.

"Um," I said, trying to think. I'm not a really quick thinker. "Well . . ." I slipped the toe shoes inside my Sack, on my desk.

Mom waited patiently. When I started going to Speech in first grade, Mom and Dad learned to wait patiently without helping or encouraging or even nodding.

"My ring," I said, holding up my left hand. My new friendship ring had slipped a little to the side, so the knot was hiding against my pinkie. I fixed it.

Mom came over and took my hand in hers. "Let me look at it again."

Of course, she had already inspected it thoroughly, as soon as she picked me up from getting them with my new best friend, Zoe Grandon, this afternoon. "It's so beautiful," Mom said again, just like she had this afternoon. I didn't mind, though. Every time I look at it, that's what I think, too. It's so beautiful.

I asked Mom, "You really think so?"

"Definitely," she said, wiggling it on my finger with her thumb over the knot. "I like that it's so strong-looking, like a boat knot — what's it called? — nautical, like you would tie with a really strong rope to hold a boat to the dock, but at the same time, it's delicate, the silver, so feminine."

I smiled at the ring. "Mmm-hmm."

"You must be so happy," Mom said softly. "I'm happy for you."

I nodded.

"Who chose it, you or Zoe?"

"Both," I said. "The other, other rings were too, I don't know — fancy. This one is just . . ."

"Perfect," Mom finished for me.

"Exactly. Yeah. So, I'll put in my ring, and . . ."

"Really?" Her eyes were open wide, like she was trying to look all innocent, but I knew what she was thinking.

"Zoe is putting hers in her bag," I explained. "She'd feel pretty stupid if I didn't."

"Uh-huh," Mom said, biting her lip.

"You . . ." I tried not to get angry.

"What?" she asked, like she didn't know.

I stamped my foot. "You . . . you're the one who-who-who didn't want me to be best friends with Morgan anymore."

"CJ!"

"What? You, you never even liked Morgan at all, you were so happy I was getting to be best friends with Zoe, and now, what? You don't want me to?"

"I didn't say anything!" Mom protested.

"Why can't you just be happy for me?"

"I am happy for you."

"But?"

Mom shrugged. "I was just imagining how Morgan might feel."

"Morgan?"

"She thinks she's still your best friend, right?"

"That's, that's not . . ." She was right, Morgan had no clue that Zoe and I had bought these rings together today.

"So how will she feel, sitting there in English when you and Zoe . . ."

I slapped my hands against my thighs, wishing I could explain or get her to stop saying that, at least.

She shook her head, bouncing her soft curls from side to side. She is so beautiful it really ticks me off sometimes.

"You just, you . . . fine. Fine!" I yelled. "You don't want me to put my ring in?"

"That's not what —"

"Fine! I won't. I won't even wear it." I pulled the ring off my finger and threw it down onto my floor. It clanked, bounced, and rolled under my bed.

"CJ," Mom said, reaching toward me.

I pulled away. "What? Does that satisfy you? You don't want me to play soccer, you don't want me to have friends, you don't want me to have any best friend except you, that's what I think!" I never talk to her like that. She looked as surprised as I felt, standing there absolutely shaking with I don't know if it was fear or rage or what.

"What?" she asked, her hands up like surrendering. "I didn't . . ."

I punched myself in the thigh. "You always keep saying I'm your best friend!"

She shrugged. "You are."

"How do you think that makes me feel?" I yelled.

"Good, I hope." She smiled a little, tilting her head.

"Yeah, except, you know what?" I asked her, starting to cry. "You're not in seventh grade! So what am I supposed to do at lunch?" I held onto my head, which felt like it might blow up.

"CJ, I think it's great that you have other friends. Really. It doesn't take away from us. I have other friends, too — Aunt Betsy, and Dad, and . . ."

"Yeah, but. . . ." It's really hard to argue with Mom. She agrees with you, which turns a person around so much, you forget what your point was. But I wasn't giving up this time, for once. "And then, then" — I wiped my eyes quickly with the heel of my hand — "then you keep saying how Morgan isn't a real friend to me."

She opened those beautiful green eyes so wide again. "I do not." My dad says he fell in love with her the minute she laid those beautiful green eyes on him.

"You do so!" I stamped my foot again. "You say it."

"CJ."

"All the time, you say it, you know you do! You make that face when I ask can she come over!"

"Morgan is here all the time," Mom protested.

I wiped my runny nose on my sleeve. "But you make that face," I said, and when she looked at me like she had no idea what I was talking about, I wanted to smash her. "Don't! You know you-you-you bite your lip and you say, 'Well, if you want to.' Right? You know you say that!" I imitated her voice. "'Well, if you want to.'"

Mom breathed out hard. She couldn't deny it.

"Right?" I asked. "And now when I'm finally like, OK, fine, so I'll be best friends with Zoe, who you think is so great, it's still not enough! I get friendship rings with Zoe, and you-you just, you don't even want me to put it in my bag! What do you want from me?"

"I just . . ."

The tears were pouring down my face. I didn't even try to wipe them. "Fine!" I yelled. "So I won't have any friends, if that's what makes you happy!"

I had to get away from her. I wanted to stomp up to my room, but we were already in my room. So I left my room and slammed the door. I stood in the hall, listening to the slam echo, thankful for the sudden silence. I've never yelled at my mother like that before. I don't think I've ever said so many sentences in a row before.

I stood there for a minute not knowing what to do. It was a sort of awkward situation. Even though I was still crying, I almost cracked a smile at the thought of Mom standing in the middle of my room, tilting her pretty head and biting her lip, not knowing what to do. Just like me, on the other side of the door. But then I realized she'd probably have to come out soon, and so I quickly slammed myself into the bathroom.

Some cold water on my face felt good. I looked at myself in the mirror — pointy nose, dark circles under my green eyes, nonexistent lips, pulled-back frizzy brown hair — and got really depressed. I'm not beautiful like my mother. I look like a gerbil. Especially when my eye rims are red from crying. Tommy must be blind or stupid or into rodents. Yuck.

After a few minutes I heard my door open. I locked the bathroom door, but Mom didn't try to come in. I heard her footsteps on the stairs going down, and then her voice in the backyard with Dad and Paul. They were all laughing, having a great time as if I didn't even matter.

three

I lay in my bed, in the dark, holding my favorite old stuffed animal. Zoe hadn't called and neither had Tommy. Luckily, neither had Morgan, because I don't know what I would've said to her.

My new friendship ring was still on the night table, where Mom had left it after our fight. She must've crawled under my bed to get it for me. Yesterday I promised Zoe I would never take it off except to put it in my Bring Yourself in a Sack. Oh, well. It was eight-thirty, and I was in bed already because I couldn't think of what else to do. My satin pillowcase felt cool against my hot face. Nobody had come to check on me.

Finally, Mom pushed my door open and came over to sit on the edge of my bed. I didn't roll over to talk with her like I usually do. She didn't say anything, just touched my forehead and pushed my hair back from it, over and over, like when I was a baby. I didn't want her to stop, so I stayed very still.

After a minute, Mom said, "I'm sorry I upset you."

I didn't answer. *Good,* I was thinking.

She stroked my head a few more times, then stood up. I listened to her footsteps crossing my floor, her slippers scratching against the wood, her long fingernails clicking as they touched my doorknob.

"What should I do?" I asked without turning around.

I heard her coming back to sit beside me again. I rolled

to face her, and she leaned over me, her hand behind my back. She smiled down at the stuffed dog clutched in my arm — History, my stop-sucking-my-thumb present from when I was two-and-a-half-years-old. I used to bring him everywhere, but most of the time lately I just leave him lined up on my shelf with the other things I'm too old for. I thought she might be about to launch into the old story of how when she handed him to me, nine years ago, she'd suggested we could call him Doggie, but I said no, his name is History. She and Dad thought I was brilliant. I always like that story, but I wasn't really in the mood. I was relieved when her smile faded quickly and she looked serious again.

I waited for her to say something. When she didn't, I buried my face in what's left of History's brown fur and asked again, "What should I do?"

"What do you think?" she asked slowly.

"I don't know! That's why I'm asking you!" I didn't mean to get mad. I never ever used to yell at her, but she's been so frustrating lately.

"OK," she said calmly. "OK, I just wondered if you'd thought of anything."

I looked up at the ceiling and didn't answer.

"Because," she continued, "I've been thinking about it, and it occurs to me, maybe this isn't nice but, well, OK. Just hear me out, but, maybe you don't need to say anything to Morgan."

"But, you said . . ."

She bit her lip and tilted her head to the side, opening her big green eyes wide. "I don't know if I'd put my ring in my Sack about Myself, but . . ."

"Bring Yourself in a Sack," I corrected.

“OK,” she said. “So maybe you don’t have to shove it in Morgan’s face that you and Zoe have become best friends, but the truth is, you have to do what’s right for you. And do you feel like being best friends with Zoe is better for you?”

“Yes,” I said.

“OK. Then, OK. I keep thinking about how happy you looked last weekend, when Zoe slept over. Hearing you girls whispering in here until I don’t know when, and giggling. You’ve seemed so much more confident and, well, happy this week. You don’t smile when you’re with Morgan.”

I sat up. “I smile.” I’m always defending Morgan to her.

“Uh-huh,” Mom said. She waited for me to keep going, if I wanted to.

I bent over my legs and buried my face between my

knees. "It's just," I whispered, "Zoe and I understand each other."

Mom didn't say anything so I turned to look at her. She was nodding.

"And she's honest, like, Morgan always has to act tough, like she doesn't care what her mother thinks or anybody, but like, Zoe — she's so funny."

"Mmm-hmm," Mom said.

I hugged my knees. "She told me about this time her mother took just her out of the five kids in her family to *Sesame Street Live* once when she was little and bought her an Elmo flashlight even though it was overpriced."

Mom nodded some more.

"And she still has it," I whispered. "And sometimes she sleeps with it under her pillow because it feels like her mother giving her attention just specially. You know? I don't think she ever told anybody but me about it."

"It's wonderful that she feels like she can confide in you," Mom whispered back.

"Exactly. And I feel like I can really talk to her, too."

"That's such a powerful bond," Mom said. "And why shouldn't you enjoy that? You're such a nice person, you would never want to purposefully hurt Morgan's feelings, but you know what? Sometimes a person has to do what's right for herself."

"That's what I think."

Mom pushed my hair back from my forehead. "And when you do what's right for yourself, things have a way of working themselves out."

"Like when you ran away from home?"

Mom looked up at my ceiling, then shook her head slowly. "That was different. It was very hard, believe me." She took a deep breath and stood up.

I wasn't quite ready for her to leave, yet. "Tommy didn't call," I said.

"I was thinking about that." She sat back down.

"It doesn't matter," I assured her. "I'll see him in school tomorrow."

She brought her shoulders up near her ears — her excited expression. When Tommy Levit called to ask me out Friday afternoon, I had barely hung up before I was jumping up and down in the kitchen. My mother ripped off her cow apron to hug me and beg for all the details, listening with her shoulders up near her ears. She let me tell her the whole Tommy conversation three times, and the pork chops burned, but she said, "Who cares, this is much more important."

"Are you nervous about it?" Mom asked.

I nodded.

"Maybe we can do a French twist in your hair. That always looks especially pretty on you," she suggested.

Usually I just wear a plain bun. Mom is the one who sometimes wears a French twist and looks especially pretty in it, but I said, "OK," hoping maybe it would look good on me, too.

"Don't scream at me," Mom whispered. "But, Tommy's the one who kissed Morgan last year, right?"

"Mmm-hmm," I said.

"Oh," said Mom without looking at me.

"She doesn't like him anymore, though," I explained. "She likes his twin brother, Jonas."

"Oh, that's fun," Mom said. She sounded relieved. She pulled her feet up to sit cross-legged on my bed. "That was a long time ago, anyway, that she kissed Tommy."

I sat up, too. "It was the day I got chosen to be a bug in *A Midsummer Night's Dream*."

Mom laughed, covering her mouth with her long, elegant fingers.

"At the time it felt like, so what, kissing. I get my toe shoes spray-painted brown."

"You stood out."

"Get kissed, be a bug. Hmm."

Mom scrunched up her nose. "Which sounds better now?"

"That's not the . . ." I said, hugging History. "There's just, a lot — so much — going on right now."

"There sure is," she agreed. "Tomorrow's a big day for you."

I nodded. She reached over and picked up my ring from the night table and handed it to me. I put it on. "Thanks," I whispered, looking again at how beautiful, how strong but delicate, my friendship ring is.

Mom pulled my covers up to my chin and tucked them tight around my body and History's. "It'll be a good day. It'll all work out," she whispered.

"Really?" I asked. "You sure?"

"I have every confidence," she said, and kissed my forehead.

four

I was up early doing my stretches and finishing my project. When I took my shower, I used double cream rinse so my hair would slick back smooth. I wanted to look good. I put on my black flared-leg Capezio pants and a gray T-shirt. While Mom was tucking my straggly hairs into a French twist, she told me I looked really cute.

"Really?"

She kissed my forehead. "Really."

Paul was using the computer, still in his pajamas, so Mom dressed him. I hate that — he's eight, not two.

Make him do something for himself. Anyway, we still got to school early. We always do, because Mom has to be at work. She goes in early so she can get out early to take me to dance.

Morgan was already at school, waiting for me sitting on the wall. She rides her bike.

"Hi!" I said. I tried to shove my ringed hand into my pocket, but my black flared Capezios have no pockets.

"Come up," Morgan said. "Did he call?"

"Who?" *Why didn't I think of a plan,* I asked myself. Mom is so stupid to say it will all work out. How? What does that mean, it will all work out? It doesn't make any sense. My head was buzzing as I climbed the wall and sat next to Morgan with my book bag on my lap, my hands hidden underneath.

"Who," Morgan repeated. "As if. Tommy!"

"No," I said. "He didn't. Not since Friday, I mean."

"Don't worry. When I went out with him last year, he never called me. Did you talk to Zoe?"

"About what?" Panic.

"About Jonas," she said impatiently.

"Oh," I said, rubbing the quilted cotton of my book bag like it could bring me luck. "Um, I-I-I, yeah. I did."

"And?"

"She, I didn't, she was going to."

"Oh, dread," Morgan said, blowing her bangs away from her eyes. "Maybe she'll ask him on the bus this morning!"

"Yeah," I said.

She grabbed me on the arms and said, "Eeee!" I almost fell off the wall. "Won't that be fun?" she asked me. "The four of us? Now if you'd just quit ballet and play soccer like a normal person, we could . . ."

"Morgan!" She's wanted me to quit since fourth grade, when she had to.

"I know, I know," she said quickly. We never really talk too much about ballet. As soon as the subject comes up, we can't even look at each other. It always feels like she's angry at me, that I didn't quit then, too. I wonder sometimes how things would be different now if we hadn't been eavesdropping that afternoon.

"It's not that I don't want to play soccer," I whispered.

"I know. Forget it. Anyway he's cute, don't you think?"

"Jonas? Yeah," I said, trying to keep my book bag balanced on my lap.

"Gawky, but in a cute way. He's sweeter than Tommy," Morgan said, blowing her long bangs out of her eyes.

"Tommy's obnoxious," I agreed.

"Jonas's hair, though."

"What?" I asked.

Morgan bit her bottom lip. "It's sort of . . ."

"I like curly hair," I assured her. "And he's so sweet."

"Too sweet, you think?" She stared into my eyes. Her eyes are so dark you can't see the pupils.

"No," I stuttered. I wiped the sweat off my forehead.

Morgan shrugged. "Anyway, the four of us could have so much fun together, as a foursome. Hey," Morgan said, grabbing my hand. "You got the ring!"

"What ring?" I asked, even though she had grabbed the only ring I had on, my new friendship ring with Zoe.

"The friendship ring!" she squealed. "This is the one we saw last week, right?"

She had been there when Zoe and I first noticed them. I swallowed. No words were coming out.

"I thought you were waiting for me," she said in her pouty way. "How much did it cost?"

"Twenty-nine dollars," I heard myself answering.

"Whoa." Morgan shook her head. Her long brown hair is straight and shiny, and she was wearing her khaki shorts and black polo shirt, her favorites. It's her look, that and sandals. Morgan has style, even my mother admits that.

"Um. . . . They have installment," I mumbled.

She smiled. "That's true," she said. "Maybe if I do some chores, my mom will give me money to put down. Do you think she'll ask him?"

"Who?"

“Zoe!” Morgan said. “Jonas!”

“Oh,” I said. “Um, yeah, probably.”

“Should I pull my hair back?” She stretched the black scrunchie she was wearing on her wrist and shook her hair off her face, to show me the pulled-back option.

“It looks good down,” I told her.

“All right. Thanks.” She smiled at me, crossed her fingers, and touched her tiny turned-up nose. It was our secret sign for being best friends. We had made it up back in fourth grade.

I made the sign back, quickly, then pulled my T-shirt away from my body a few times to give myself some air. It was an awfully hot day, for mid-September.

“Here they are!” Morgan pointed at the bus rumbling into the circle. It had a big letter B on it, so I knew who was inside. “Do I look OK?” Morgan asked. “Be honest.”

She gritted her teeth so I could inspect them. She has a terror of something being caught between her teeth — she brushes at least three times every day, with plain baking soda sometimes, which made me gag when I tried it at her house. Morgan told me, "Stick with it, you can get used to anything."

"You look great," I said. "You could do a toothpaste commercial."

She shoved me lightly. Then we both turned to watch the B bus's door creak open. She blew at her bangs again, then shook her hair back from her face. It looked very cool, how she did that.

A few sixth graders got off the bus first, then Jonas and Tommy Levit. Jonas looked over at us and smiled, but Tommy headed straight for the upper playground where some boys were playing Cream the Carrier. He has the straightest eyebrows, I noticed. They make him look so serious and intense.

"Jonas really does walk like a chicken," Morgan whispered. "Doesn't he?"

"Tommy's high-tops are untied," I said.

Morgan flicked her hair back again and whispered, "We're so bad."

Another couple of kids got off. *Maybe Zoe will be absent*, I thought and wished. I had found ten items this morning besides my ring for my Bring Yourself in a Sack. I could just avoid the whole thing, and Mom would end up being right — it would all work out.

Just as I was praying that, though, Zoe stepped off the bus. I saw her look around for us, her dirty-blond hair tucked behind her ears, her oversize T-shirt hanging loosely down over her jeans.

“Hey!” Zoe yelled when she spotted us. She waved, and I saw that her friendship ring was right there on her finger.

I jumped down and said “Hi!” I crossed my arms over my chest, hoping Zoe would do the same, but instead she was actually playing with her ring — wiggling it around with her thumb looped under her two middle fingers to get at it. The boys on the upper playground could notice that ring.

Morgan jumped down and stood next to us.

“So,” I said quickly to Zoe. “Did you say anything to Jonas?”

“Like what?” she asked. She hiked her backpack up on her shoulder and played with her ring again. “I mean, they’re at my bus stop.” Her hand looked huge to me; I couldn’t take my eyes off it.

"No," I said, smiling at her and leaning in close. "About Morgan."

Zoe looked at Morgan, so I did, too. She was staring at her perfectly turned-out feet in their clunky sandals. Morgan wears sandals until November.

"Oh," Zoe said. "Not yet. But listen, Morgan, my sister said yes, you can have her old cleats for soccer. Size five, right?"

"Yeah," Morgan mumbled, without looking up. My stomach lurched.

The bell to go in rang.

"I'll bring them in tomorrow," Zoe told her.

Morgan shrugged. I tried to think of what to do. She saw it, obviously. She saw Zoe's ring, and I was stuck there between them, unable to disappear.

Zoe shrugged at me.

I had to say something, so I asked Zoe, "You'll ask Jonas?" My voice sounded cracky and far away.

Zoe tilted her head and said, "Sure."

"Don't," Morgan said.

"What?" Zoe asked. "You changed your mind already?" She smiled at me and then at Morgan and then back at me. She has the friendliest smile — you can see her molars; it makes you have to smile back.

Kids were passing us going in to school. "You coming?" Olivia Pogostin asked us.

I nodded and looked up at my book bag on the wall, next to Morgan's. "Zoe?" I asked. "Could you grab mine and Morgan's bags? We're too short." Morgan and I used to share a chair at each other's kitchen tables, and her mother would say look at the Tinies! A little pair of Tinies! It was a sort of thing with us, being little. I wanted to show her we're still friends.

Morgan didn't smile back. She glanced at Zoe, then grabbed her own bag. I guess she's grown a lot since last year. "I can get my own," she said.

Zoe pulled my bag down and, handing it to me, said, "I'll try to talk to Jonas today."

"No," Morgan said. "I hate him. He walks like a chicken. Ew." She walked fast into school, yelling, "Hey, Olivia — wait up!" Zoe and I shrugged at each other and followed her in. My legs felt like two hundred pounds each.

five

Permission slips for apple picking were handed out in homeroom. "Yes!" Lou Hochstetter said when he got his. "Apple picking!"

"Ah," said Ms. Cress. "Something excites Lou besides World War Two artillery?"

"I like other stuff," Lou protested. "I like, um . . ."

"Yes?" asked Ms. Cress. She's always about to laugh, which I think is unusual for a math/science teacher. But she's also really young, like twenty-something, and she wears short skirts with boots — except when she's coaching the girls' soccer team, when she wears sneakers, short-shorts, and T-shirts. All the boys come to soccer games at least partly because they're all in love with her. It would be typical of Lou to say, "I like you!"

But he didn't. Even Lou isn't that bold. He said, "Um . . ."

"Hay-stacking!" Gideon Weld coughed into his hands.

"I like the Internet," Lou said, sinking into his chair. He's the tallest boy in our grade and sort of a doof, but also funny. His mother is running for mayor. "And I like apple picking."

Ms. Cress raised her eyebrows, twice, and said, "Mmm-hmm." We all knew what she was thinking about. "Work with me, people," she said. She wrote the information on the board for us to fill in the blanks of our permission slips.

I love trips, and I've been looking forward to this one for six years. It's tradition at Boggs Middle that the seventh grade starts out the year going apple picking. It's supposed to promote unity. Last year on the trip, two couples got caught making out behind a haystack. The whole school found out, of course, including Ms. Cress and every other teacher. "Hay-stacking" immediately became our new dirty word. The two couples were practically movie stars for a week. We mostly say making out or scooping, now, but "hay-stacking" still means a romantic, forbidden kind of kissing. Nobody says it out loud — you sort of have to clear your throat with it: "Hay-stacking."

"Oh, no," I heard myself groan when Ms. Cress wrote Monday, September 21, on the board.

“Something wrong, CJ?” Ms. Cress asked.

I shook my head, but then asked, “What time will we get back?”

“Six-thirty,” Ms. Cress said and wrote at the same time. “Now that’s a week from today, ’K? So we need these permission slips back pronto!”

I rested my face in my hands all through the announcements. Even after the bell rang, while Ms. Cress was yelling, “And, hey, really try to get these permission slips back to me fast — we’ve got a contest going in the teacher’s lunchroom, and I want to win the cookie!” I didn’t look up. She thinks she’s hip, such a kid. Teachers should just realize they are adults.

I finally folded my permission slip, stuck it into my bag, and headed toward Spanish. Zoe, who takes French, was outside Madame F's door, hanging out chatting with Olivia.

"Is your hip hurting?" Olivia asked me.

"My what?"

"Your hip," she repeated. "You're rubbing it."

"Oh," I said, realizing I was still searching for a nonexistent pocket. "Um, a little. But, I mean, no." Olivia's mother and mine are number one on each other's speed dial, so everything gets back, fast.

"That's good," Olivia said, twirling one of her pigtails.

"Thanks," I said.

Tommy passed us, going to Spanish. On his way, he said, sort of in my direction, "Hi."

Zoe and I looked at each other. I could feel myself blushing so I covered my face with my hands.

Olivia asked, "What?"

I expected Zoe to explain, but when I looked up, she was staring at her friendship ring, readjusting it. So I told Olivia, "Tommy asked me out."

"Oh," Olivia said. I couldn't tell what she was thinking. She's really sweet in some ways, but she has strong opinions. I think I let her down sometimes. "When?" she asked.

"Friday," I said.

"Congratulations." She opened her folder holder and flipped through.

"Thanks," I said again. We're more cousins than friends, Olivia and I. In fact, I call her mom Aunt Betsy. She's one of the few not-totally-white kids around, because her father is half-black and her mother is half-Filipino. Over the summer some kids at the Swim Club whispered, "Kung Fu," right in front of us at the snack bar. Olivia said, "So what, they're showing their ignorance," but I wanted to punch their ignorant teeth in. Mom said I had good instincts; she didn't blame me. When I was in *The Nutcracker* last year, Olivia gave me a good-luck flip book she made herself of a ballerina doing a leap and then a pirouette, which was amazing and obviously took her forever to make no matter how talented she is. But even though we really do care about each other, we're very different — she still wants to invent board games together and send them to be patented. I'm ready to talk about boys. She's much more of a brain so I feel stupid, sometimes, like when I bring home a test with an 87 and my dad says that's great, what did Olivia get, 101? It's a joke, but still, sometimes it's hard to figure out how to act toward her.

She slid her permission slip into one of her folders and asked me, "So you can't go on the trip, huh?"

"What?" Zoe asked. "Why?"

Morgan was just passing us, going to Spanish, but she said, "Dance."

"Hey, wait up," I called to her. We usually walk together.

Zoe and Olivia followed us. "What is she talking about?" Zoe asked me.

"I can't go apple picking," I said.

"Why not?" Zoe asked. Her voice is so loud.

"We don't get back until six-thirty," Olivia told her.

"Yeah? So?"

"So," said Morgan, stopping outside Spanish. I almost bumped into her. "CJ has dance at four on Mondays. Not that she even likes ballet anymore, but . . ."

Olivia looked at me. "You don't?"

"It's complicated," I answered. I dropped my book bag and checked my French twist. It was holding, of course — my mom is so good at hair she does everybody's for performances.

"You like it or you don't," Morgan said, blowing her bangs out of her eyes. "How complicated is that?"

"You can't miss one day?" Zoe asked me quietly.

I shook my head. "Something could happen, some casting director could come to watch. You can't. And especially, my mother?"

Morgan blew her long, dark bangs out of her eyes again and explained, "CJ's mother says it's important to devote yourself to something so you'll stand out from the crowd." She used a high voice like my mother's. Morgan is a good actress so it really did sound like Mom.

“Really?” Zoe asked me. “She says that?”

“All the time,” Morgan answered. “Makes me feel great.”

“She doesn’t mean anything against you,” I told her. Morgan thinks my mother looks down on her. She doesn’t, not really. “She just, it’s true that . . .”

“My mother says it’s important to clean your nails,” Zoe said.

We all laughed. Zoe is good at breaking the tension. She has four older sisters, so she gets practice.

“That’s why CJ is a superstar, and I have three nail clippers,” Zoe added.

I shook my head. “Don’t say that.” The last thing I need is my new best friend calling me a star, too, thinking I’m a show-off. I just want to be normal, one of the crowd, like her.

"What?" Zoe asked. "Not that you don't have clean nails or anything. I'm sure your nails are clean."

"I meant, I'm not even close to a superstar," I explained. "At all. If my dance friend Fiona ever heard me called a star she would get a good laugh — I fall out of my turns."

"Fiona is a boring bimbo," Morgan said.

I had to laugh. "That's true." Morgan, Fiona, and I had been the three best in Level One. Morgan had the best turn-out, Fiona had the best arches, and I had the longest neck. We envied one another's parts.

"So who cares what Fiona thinks," Zoe said. "The bimbo." All four of us were smiling. Poor Fiona.

I shook my head. "I really wanted to go apple picking."

"Or at least hay-stacking," Zoe coughed.

Olivia scrunched her face and said, "Yuck."

"I like apples," I protested.

"Yeah, apples," Zoe said, grinning. "An apple a day."

The bell rang. "Uh-oh," Zoe said. "I'm dead."

Morgan grabbed Olivia's arm and asked, "It's so pathetic, don't you think, when all some girls obsess about is boys, boys, boys?"

Olivia looked up at me for a second but then nodded at Morgan. "I do," she said. Zoe ran down the hall toward French, and I followed Morgan and Olivia into Spanish.

six

Morgan left Spanish before I got my stuff together and was already in her seat by the time I got back to Ms. Cress's for math/science. I felt like throwing up. She looked so serious and sad. I passed her a note saying, "I'm sorry. Please, please, please don't be mad."

"About what?" she wrote back. Then she passed a note to Olivia, and I saw Olivia turn around and nod at Morgan before she glanced back at me.

After math/science, Morgan was out of her seat and the room before the bell finished ringing.

"Wait up," I called to her, grabbing my stuff. "Hey!" It's not like she could avoid me. We have every period except eighth together. "Morgan!"

She turned around. So did everybody in the hall. I had been yelling. "What?" she whispered, looking around.

I opened my mouth but nothing came out. My right knee wouldn't stop wobbling, so I had to rest that foot on top of the other. "It's-it's-it's not what you think," I started to explain.

"What isn't?" Morgan took a drink from the water fountain. Tommy passed by going to his locker but didn't look at me.

"The friendship rings," I whispered. I hadn't come up with a plan. All I could think was, *Please, words, please come out in some order that will make her stop looking so angry.*

"I don't care," she said, staring me right in the eyes. That's just how she talks to her dad the few times he calls. Yeah, uh-huh, I don't care, 'bye.

"Morgan."

"Olivia's waiting for me." She turned around and went to the lockers. It was pretty obvious she didn't want me to go, too, and my locker is right down the row from hers, so I didn't know what to do. I leaned against the wall and tried not to cry.

Everything had been going so well: I'm in Level Three, I have an amazing best friend wearing a friendship ring with me, and an adorable, sarcastic boyfriend. Nobody could wish for a better start to seventh grade, except maybe please, please, please don't let it all crash into bits like it's doing now.

My eyes were closed as I pressed into fifth position trying to concentrate on just that, just turn-out, when Zoe tapped me on the forehead. I opened my eyes.

"Hey," she said, smiling at me.

I buried my face in my hands.

"Come on," she said and dragged me to the bathroom.

"What am I going to do?" I sank down along the wall onto the cold bathroom floor. "Morgan hates me. She's so hurt and it's my fault, with all she's going through at home, I should never, I-I feel so terrible."

Zoe twisted the friendship ring on her finger so the knot part was hidden in her palm and asked, "What did she say?"

"Nothing. 'I don't care.' 'What are you talking about?' You know." I bent over my legs and buried my face in my calves. "Argh."

"Did she say something or did you?" Zoe asked.

"I did." I looked up at her. "I just, I felt like, I mean it was obvious that she, so . . . What? Was that really stupid of me? I mean, what, I should just, what? Ignore it?"

"I don't know." Zoe sat down next to me.

"My mother said don't say anything, just, you know. Don't make a big, but, I-I-I how can I just, I mean . . ."

"Maybe you don't need to keep apologizing to her, though."

I shrugged. "But . . ."

"It just might, you know, make her feel worse. Maybe."

"Maybe," I said, closing my eyes.

Zoe pulled at her shoelace, unraveling it. "I don't know."

"No," I agreed. "You're probably right."

"I don't know," Zoe said again. "I just know, the longer I can avoid a conflict, the better."

"Yeah," I said, wiping my nose with my palm. "Me, too."

We sat there for a second, not talking. An eighth-grade girl came in and almost tripped on us, going to the stall. We both pulled our legs in close to our bodies and smiled at each other. "I feel like we live here," Zoe whispered. Last week she was crying in the bathroom; now it was me. She picked at a callus on her hand while the eighth grader flushed, came out, and left without washing her hands. We made faces at each other like, gross! Then we laughed.

"You OK?" Zoe asked.

I nodded and put my chin down on my knees. The bathroom floor was so hard and cold and probably full of gross germs. "Much better," I said. "Thanks."

She half-shrugged, one shoulder only. So what if she's a little big in the rear? She has a very pretty face, very photogenic. Morgan was saying last week that Zoe has such nice blue eyes, it's too bad she's a little big in the rear. Maybe boys think that — Morgan said boys like really little butts — but I think they should notice Zoe's eyes and her sense of humor. I worried, actually, last week that maybe Zoe and Tommy liked each other. There were strange silences between them. But I guess not, because she got him to ask me out.

"Tommy barely said hello to me," I whispered.

Zoe went over to the sink and turned on the water. "He wouldn't have asked you out if he didn't like you."

"I guess. Hey!" I stood up, excited. "Maybe Morgan will feel better if you get Jonas to ask her out. What do you think? Because she's been saying wouldn't it be fun, the four of us could —"

"Fun," Zoe said, pressing up on the soap dispenser so many times the pink ooze overflowed her palm.

"I am such a jerk." I turned around and banged my head against the wall. "I'm sorry. I'm sorry. I should just shut up like my mother says to."

"No," Zoe said, scrubbing. "It's just like, wa-hoo, that would be really fun for me, you four."

"What about if we fix you up with somebody, too?"

"Yeah," she said, rinsing. "Like who?"

I thought for a sec. "Lou."

"Lou?" she asked. "Lou Hochstetter?"

"What's wrong with Lou? He's in my homeroom."

"Lou." She kept rinsing her hands. No wonder her fingernails are so clean. "Lou?"

I started to laugh, how she was saying that. "What?"

"Mr. World War Two."

"He's tall."

"Maybe you *should* shut up, actually," Zoe suggested.

I handed her a paper towel. "Think about it?"

"Shut up." She pointed at me, but she was smiling.

"Fine."

"No, actually, that'll be great, since you can't come apple picking," she said, rubbing each finger dry with the paper towel. "Yeah. Me and Lou, we'll be hay-stacking next week while you pirouette, or whatever. Great."

I slumped back down. "You're gonna have so much fun."

"I am NOT hay-stacking Lou Hochstetter. Hello! Joke!"

"No," I said. "I don't even, no, I just, you're all gonna

be, even if nobody hay-stacks at all, it's like, OK, I can't play soccer, but now . . . Everybody will be, unifying, while I sit outside the principal's office, waiting to be picked up for dance. No way. Forget it. I quit."

"Quit what?"

"Ballet," I said. "Last year I was happy to be a bug, this year I want to be normal."

"A bug?" Zoe asked. "What?"

I shook my head. "Nothing. Just, I'm quitting ballet."

She crumpled the paper towel and leaned against the wall. "Maybe you could just get out of Monday. You don't have to be so drastic."

"No, she'll never let me," I tried to explain. "And anyway it's not just Monday. It's like, what I really want, I mean, I explained it to you. Remember?" It's what I had confided to her, at our sleepover.

Zoe nodded. "You want to hang around at the pizza place."

"You make it sound idiotic," I complained. "It's not about pizza, it's just, like . . ." I grabbed my foot and stretched it over my head. Stretching helps me think.

"Youch," she said. She grabbed her foot and tried to pull it up, but it only got about up to her waist before she lost her balance.

I smiled and put my foot down. "It's not just apple picking either. It's the whole, I want to slouch. I want to watch TV all day on Saturday."

"There's nothing on."

"I want to be on the soccer team."

"That would be fun," Zoe admitted.

"Wouldn't it? I mean, I like performing but, I don't know." I pictured crossing the stage in a series of leaps, my legs long and straight, graceful as a swan. I shook my head. "I like it OK, but maybe not as much as like, being part of everybody. Going out for pizza after games."

"Bunch of lunatics smooshed in a booth, rehashing the game, grabbing slices" — Zoe nodded — "that's the best."

"It is. And she's the one — my mom, she's like — 'You have to do what's right for you.'"

Zoe pitched the paper towel into the wastebasket. "Well, that's true."

"Yes. Definitely. So too bad on my mother. When she wanted something different, she just, she was buying apple butter, but she didn't, she j-j-j-j . . ."

"What?"

I took a deep breath. I rarely stutter, anymore — only

when I get really nervous or upset, or if I have to say my name in front of people. That's still hard. In first grade I got stuck on the *S* sound every morning; it was dreadful. Some kids teased me about it, called me C-C-C instead of CJ. The only ones who didn't were Morgan, Zoe, and Olivia — which I'll never forget.

I looked up at Zoe. She was watching me, playing with her friendship ring. She smiled, then. She really uses her whole face, doing it. I don't know anybody else who smiles so big like that. "You really want to do soccer?" she asked.

"Yeah," I said, trying to sound sure. "I'm gonna quit."

"That's great," Zoe said, picking up her bag.

I picked up mine and asked, "Is it?"

"So great." Zoe pushed the bathroom door open. "We can go for pizza after practice tomorrow."

"That'd be excellent."

"And we can sit together on the bus to apple picking," Zoe offered, holding open the cafeteria door.

"Great," I said. The smell-combination of mashed potatoes and chocolate pudding was nauseating. "Listen, Zoe? Can you come to dance with me after school today? For moral support, to tell my mother? Because she, I don't know what she'll say."

"Today?"

"It's too short notice, right? Never mind."

"No," she said. "I don't care about that."

"Oh. I have a quarter if you want to call your mom and ask. Unless you have plans with somebody else."

"No," she said. "I have no life, and my mom won't care. Oops." She bent down to retie her shoelace.

"Great, then."

I didn't want to stare at our table, where Morgan and Olivia were whispering together, so I casually glanced around. Gideon Weld was signalling me and Zoe to come over to the boys' table. Tommy pushed him. Obviously, my boyfriend didn't want me at his table. Oh, well. I don't need him watching me chew.

"You're so lucky," I whispered to Zoe, as she stood up.

"You're the one Tommy wants to sit with," she said, looking toward the boys' table.

I felt myself blushing. "He does not, either." I hoped I was wrong and Zoe was right — that maybe Tommy was just shy but really wanted to be with me.

Zoe shrugged. We sat down at the other end of Morgan's table. She looked at us, then whispered something to Olivia.

"And anyway," I whispered to Zoe. "I meant, that you

can just do what you want, without your mother getting all, involved."

Zoe shrugged again and ripped open her lunch bag. "I'm the fifth kid," she explained. "By the time I came around, my parents were like, oh, just put her out in the backyard with the others."

I looked down the table at Morgan, who cupped her hand over Olivia's ear. "Hey," I whispered to Zoe. "Um, do you think, maybe we shouldn't put our friendship rings in our Bring Yourself in a Sack."

She looked down at her friendship ring and covered the knot with her thumb.

"Just because" — I tilted my head toward Morgan — "you know. A lot's going on with her at home, and we don't need to shove it in her face."

"Oh, sure," Zoe agreed, nodding. "No big deal."

"Thanks," I whispered.

She held out her baggie of homemade cookies. I almost said no thanks, but then, to celebrate my new normal life, I ate one. I don't normally eat cookies, because to be graceful as a swan you can't let yourself get chubby. Sometimes when I get bored during barre exercises I say cookie names in rhythm: Nutter Butter Oreo Chips Ahoy Deluxe. I bit into Zoe's cookie smiling, like, *Ha! I'm regular! I play soccer. I eat cookies.*

It didn't taste as good as I'd expected.

seven

My mother saw us and beeped. Beeped and beeped. Zoe waved. She hopped toward the car, holding her sneaker, because for her emergency tenth thing in her Bring Yourself in a Sack in place of her friendship ring, she had taken the frayed shoelace out of her sneaker and explained, "This is because I am barely holding myself together." Everybody had laughed. Her project was definitely the funniest — she even had a piece of French toast in there to show her family's favorite food. Mine was just so boring — this is my toe shoe, these are exercise bands, this is a program from

The Nutcracker. All dance stuff except History, who I threw in this morning as my tenth thing. If I really do quit ballet, I thought, maybe I'll be less boring, like Zoe and Tommy and Morgan. Even Olivia had all different kinds of things — charcoal pencils, a calculator, soccer ball earrings, a dictionary, a pool ball. I was so embarrassed.

"Hi, Zoe!" Mom yelled out the window. I want my friends and Mom to like one another. It was always a hard part about Morgan, that Mom thinks she's an angry person — that's what she says, but I sort of worry that maybe Mom is just a snob. Mom says no, it's not her house or her shoes, she only worries that Morgan hurts my feelings. Which is true. It's a relief that Mom thinks I'm making a good choice of Zoe as a best friend.

"How did it go?" Mom whispered when I opened the front door.

"Fine," I whispered back.

She smiled and said, "Great. I knew it. OK, come on — we're really going to have to speed this time!"

"Zoe wanted to come," I said, not getting in yet. "Her mother said it's OK."

A lie — she didn't even call. It just popped out. Mom would just never understand that not every mother is like her. I'm sure Zoe's mother had no idea what Zoe was bringing in her Sack — or even that she got a friendship ring. So I lied and waited for the consequences. I tightened every muscle of my body.

"I'd be happy for the company," Mom said, still smiling. "But it might be sort of boring for Zoe, just to sit there with me — are you sure you want to, Zoe?"

"I, um, yeah!" Zoe said.

I relaxed my muscles. That wasn't so hard, I decided. "I'll sit in back with Zoe," I told Mom. "Is that OK?"

"Of course," Mom said. "By the way, Zoe — I love your rings."

"Thank you," Zoe said. "Me, too."

I slammed the front door, opened the back, and slid across the seat. Zoe and I smiled at each other as I tossed my ballet bag into the front passenger seat. I took a deep breath.

"You can do it," Zoe whispered to me.

I twisted my friendship ring around my finger for luck before I started. "Mom?"

"Do you have enough room to stretch back there?" Mom asked. "I can move up a little." She pulled a lever and yanked her seat forward by wiggling her behind.

“I’m fine,” I answered. “You don’t have to squish.”

“Here, let me dig out your stuff.” She steered with her knee so she could unzip my ballet bag. She’s always doing things for me; it’s embarrassing.

“You don’t have to —”

“We won’t really have time for stretching when you get there,” she interrupted. “And the last thing you need with *The Nutcracker* auditions coming up is an injury.” She tossed my dance clothes back. I caught them before they hit Zoe.

I yanked off my shorts. I always change in the car, on the way, but it was a little awkward, with Zoe there. I held my T-shirt out to cover me as I pulled down my underpants. I got them off and my tights on in one motion.

“Um, Mom?” It’s hard for me to talk and struggle my leotard on, under my T-shirt, at the same time.

"What? I can't hear you," Mom said. "Talk louder. Did something happen today?"

"No, I just . . ." I straightened my leotard's skinny straps and pulled on my new leg warmers; I decided not to feel guilty about wearing them even if I'm quitting because sometimes nondancers wear leg warmers just to be cozy. I could still wear them. And they're such a soft pink, anybody would feel pretty inside them.

"What?" Mom asked, turning around.

"Please watch the road, Mom." I hate when she turns around, driving.

Mom smiled at Zoe as if they were the best friends and I was the overprotective mother, then turned the right way. I took a deep breath and stretched my neck.

Mom beeped at the car in front of us as the light was turning green. "This rushing, it's crazy. I should just get you out of eighth period — you don't need gym or band. You get plenty of culture and exercise from ballet. And the last thing you want to be doing is running around, twisting your ankles. It could ruin you for the season."

"I don't run, Mom."

"She doesn't," Zoe added, backing me up. "She's very careful of her ankles. Honestly."

I saw Mom smile quickly in the rearview mirror. "Well, good. But I'm going to ask for a conference with Mrs. Johnson, see what I can do."

"Mom, please don't talk to the principal." I couldn't look at Zoe. Kids at school used to say I got special privileges, because my mother kept going in to talk to the principal. No wonder people didn't like me.

"What?" Mom asked innocently. "I'll just explain to

her that since you are a serious ballerina, you can't risk twisting an ankle."

"Mom," I begged. "Please. Nobody in the whole school gets out of gym except Ken Carpenter."

"Who's Ken Carpenter?"

"You remember. The genius who goes to the high school for calculus eighth period, he's so brilliant, even smarter than Olivia. Nobody sits with him at lunch."

"CJ!"

"What? It's true! Isn't it, Zoe?"

"Yeah," Zoe admitted. "He's way beyond us."

"Well, there's no shame in standing out, being special." Mom swerved around a slow car in the left lane. "I'm sure Ken Carpenter's mother is very proud of him. Am I right, Zoe?"

"I don't really know Mrs. Carpenter," Zoe said. "She seems proud, I guess."

As Mom swerved back into the left lane, Zoe buckled her seat belt. How embarrassing. My mother, the wild woman.

"What I mean is," Mom said, "it's important to devote yourself to something, so you'll stand out from the crowd." I mouthed the words along with her, which made Zoe smile. Mom saw her smile and added, "I guess your mother tells you the same thing, huh, Zoe?"

"Well," Zoe answered. "Actually, my mom, not really. But then, I have no talents, so the whole subject doesn't really come up."

"Mom?" I interrupted. "Mom? I think I want to, um, stop, for a while, to, I know you want me to and I made a commitment, but it's, soccer starts tomorrow and I-I-I —"

A siren wailed behind us.

"Um," Zoe said. "I think, excuse me?"

"No, no, no," Mom said, checking her rearview mirror. "OK, CJ? Lean back and start crying."

"What?"

"And hold your nose. No! Your ear!" She pulled slowly over to the side of the road. Spinning red lights flashed through the back window over us. I leaned against the window with my hand cupped on my ear, not daring to look at Zoe as footsteps approached us, crunching in the gravel.

Mom opened her window and started talking fast. "I'm so glad you found us, Officer."

“What seems to be the trouble, ma’am?” he asked. I looked at his uniform out my window. He had a gun and handcuffs attached to his belt.

“It’s my daughter, CJ,” Mom said sweetly. “She’s in pain.”

I ducked my head lower and prayed Zoe wouldn’t crack up, or we’d be going to jail. Just what we need with *The Nutcracker* auditions coming up, I could imagine my mother saying as the prison gate slams.

“What happened?” the police officer asked. “You left me in your dust, forty-five M-P-H through that red light.”

I stared at his gun. In England the cops don’t carry guns. I wished we were in England instead of Massachusetts.

“It’s her ear, Officer,” my mother said sweetly. I hate

when she uses that voice, like when she's talking to the principal. It embarrasses me, the way she tilts her head and goes soprano. "A Q-tip accident."

I pushed my head hard into the cool window to keep from turning to look at Mom and saying, "What?"

"Is it bleeding?"

"Well, it was," Mom explained.

He leaned in Mom's window and looked at me. "Are you in pain, sweetheart?"

"No," I croaked. *I hate her,* I thought, feeling the pain of embarrassment at my weird mother burning a path from my stomach right up to the back of my tongue. I hate the lying witch. She used to knit me and herself matching outfits and have my father take pictures of us wearing them in the backyard. She still dresses my brother for school even though he's eight. She sometimes gets a poppy seed caught between her front teeth. Hate, disgust. It was hard to believe I could ever tolerate the sight of her. All of which is new. Until last month, I thought she was perfect — the most beautiful, glamorous, perfect woman, exactly the person I was aiming to be when I grow up.

"We were just kidding around," Zoe said.

My mother spun around and shot Zoe a look.

"And I pushed her arm," Zoe added. "I didn't mean to hurt her."

"Well, you have to be careful," said the policeman. "Ears are very fragile. Did you know there are more bones in your ear than in your foot?"

"I didn't know that," Zoe said. "I'll be more careful."

"It's feeling better, then?" the officer asked me.

"Yes." I couldn't look at any of them, like the three of

them were joining forces to humiliate me, to make me feel a step and a half behind. *Ha, ha, ha, hope you're all having a great time lying at my expense.* I felt the tears start to come, hot tears of hatred for every person in the whole world.

"Then I guess I can relax," Mom told him. "What a relief. Do you have kids, Officer?"

"No, but my sister is deaf," he answered.

"Oh," said Mom. "So you understand."

"Sure do. Ears." He shook his head. I closed my eyes.

Mom smiled. "You should be a psychologist. I feel so much calmer just having talked to you." I hate that voice she uses. Hate, hate, hate.

"That's what my mother tells me," he said, hiking up his gun belt. "It's funny you say that, too."

"Well," said Mom, "you should always listen to your mother. Right, CJ?"

I think I said right, or maybe I just grunted. I couldn't take much more. Mom and her pal the police guy said their good-byes, and he warned her to be careful. It was like they were old friends from college or something. He went back to his car and waved as he passed us, getting back into traffic.

"Mom!"

She was checking her lipstick in the rearview mirror, wiping a smudge of it off her front tooth. How mortifying, how totally horrible. "Great job, Zoe," she said.

Zoe was grinning ear to ear as Mom put the car into gear and we barreled down the road. "That was awesome," Zoe said.

"Yeah," Mom agreed. "Awesome."

Zoe leaned forward between the two front seats and said, "You are the coolest mother."

Mom laughed, totally thrilled, and said, "In your dust! Can you believe some people?"

"Hardly," I answered, shaking my head. I gathered my strength, because now was the perfect time to disappoint all her plans for me, my career, my life. "Mom?"

"Are you stretching, CJ? We're so late."

"Mom, I just, I—" I grabbed my feet and bent my head to them. I knew what she would say if I brought up soccer, *But you're so talented, blah, blah, blah.* What she doesn't understand is maybe I don't care about talent. Maybe there's only room in each family for one superstar, and in ours, Mom's obviously got that part. I know I'm a lot better at ballet than soccer. But even if I just sit on the bench most of the time, like last year, at least I'd be sitting with my friends. Mom would never want to just sit on the sidelines, but maybe, maybe I do.

"What?" Mom asked.

I took a deep breath. "The apple-picking trip is for next Monday."

"Oh! Do they need class mothers? I could get out of work. But, wait, will we be back in time?"

"No, not until six-thirty. But I really, really want to go. The whole point is to unify the seventh grade, so I *have* to go." I pressed my knees away from each other, onto the velour of the car seat. Zoe was looking out the window, grinning.

"Of course you want to," Mom said. "I'd love to go, myself. I love apple picking."

"But no, it's not your, this is my, if I don't go I won't be part of-of-of anything. The whole seventh grade will be unified without me."

Zoe ripped open an M&M's packet, took a few, then passed it to me. I was about to say no thanks when I realized, I can! Mom can't control even what I eat. I have a right to be a normal kid, just a part of the seventh grade. A normal kid would eat the M&M's.

I poured seven of them into my hand and slammed them into my mouth. One went straight down my throat. I lurched forward, gagging.

"What's wrong?" Mom asked frantically. "You OK?" She almost swerved off the road.

"Mom!"

"Are you choking?"

"I'm fine."

"What are you eating?"

"M&M's," I said nastily, with my mouth full.

"I have some cut-up apples for you."

"I hate apples," I said.

Zoe kicked me. She was grinning.

I thought at first she was as surprised as I was that I would speak in that tone of voice to my mother, but then she whispered, "I thought you love apples."

I almost choked on my M&M's again. "Unless they're fresh picked," I said.

"Hmm," Zoe said, handing me the M&M's. As I took a few from the package, she coughed, "Hay-stacking," into her hands, just like Gideon Weld had this morning. It's the way everybody did it last year so we wouldn't get in trouble. The whole school sounded like we were coming down with bronchitis.

"Well, that's OK," Mom said.

"What is?" I asked. For a horrified second I thought she meant hay-stacking.

"A few M&M's aren't going to make you fat," she said. "You don't need an eating disorder."

I rolled up the package. I didn't want the M&M's anymore, once she said I could have them. The whole point was to rebel, although, I don't want to get fat and ugly and make her think I have no self-control. She'd be disappointed in me, I'd be too ugly to look at. But I don't want an eating disorder, because that would disappoint her, too — or maybe I should get an eating disorder just to have my own something, once in my life.

I handed the M&M's to Zoe, who was still grinning to herself, as if she'd practically caught me hay-stacking. I smiled at her, shaking my head. I had told Mom about those kids hay-stacking last year, of course — I tell her everything. My life doesn't completely happen to me until I've described it all to my mother.

When I looked up, Mom smiled her perfect smile at me in the rearview mirror, like she was in on what was cracking up me and Zoe. It burned the insides of my cheeks, wondering if she can read my mind about wanting to kiss Tommy. If I do, if I someday kiss Tommy, maybe I won't tell her. She'd probably know, anyway, somehow. She always does.

"Hey," she said. "Maybe Daddy and I could take you apple picking Sunday, you and Paul, the whole family? Wouldn't that be fun?"

"Fun," I muttered. She thinks I'm eight years old.

"And maybe Zoe could come! What do you think, Zoe?"

Before Zoe got pulled in, I said, "That's not the point, Mom. The point is not apples!"

"I know it's hard, Seej. You make so many sacrifices for ballet, don't you? And you were really looking forward to this trip."

The M&M's had left a sour taste in my mouth, but no way was I asking for her cut-up apples — especially if she wasn't even taking me seriously about going apple picking. She wasn't even considering it. So unfair. "I'm sick of sacrifices," I grumbled. "I just want to be regular."

"No, you don't," Mom said.

"How do you know what I want?" It was such a rude thing to say I was shocked at myself. I felt my eyes opening really wide. *She should punish me for that,* I thought.

She turned off the radio. My body tightened, waiting.

"I know you, CJ," she said quietly. "I know you've always been happiest while you're dancing. You have a natural gift most people would die for. I would die for it. And for your opportunities."

I pictured her as a kid, kneeling beside a cow, bargaining with God to trade anything for a chance like mine.

"For your talent, and opportunities, especially combined with your perfect ballet body —"

"Mom!"

"It's true. But it's not enough. There's a commitment involved, CJ, right? And if you're not willing to make it, there are plenty of other talented girls who will." We'd had a big discussion in August. Tchaikovsky was playing on the stereo at the time and we'd just come home from the exhausting full-day tryouts, when I got accepted into Level Three. I was wiped out and relieved and excited; it felt like, just a little more hard work, and maybe it really could be me in the spotlight someday. I had danced well that day. Yes, yes, I'm sure, I'd insisted, stretching on the living room floor. I want it. So I watched Mom sign the check for this season. *You are just like your mother,* Dad said proudly. *So determined.*

Mom's voice was low and quiet, now. "It was your choice, CJ."

"I know," I said. I smoothed the hair back from my forehead and closed my eyes again.

Mom's eyes flicked up to the rearview mirror. I looked down at the new leg warmers she'd gotten me. Pink, my favorite — a present for the new season. "I know it's hard sometimes," Mom said. "But you have to be dedicated if you want to excel."

When I was little and fighting with her, she used to say, *Fine, it's your choice — do whatever you please.* I hated that,

I still hate that, because as soon as she says that, it makes me have to do whatever she wants. “I know,” I said again, pulling the leg warmers down over my feet.

“Do you want me to call Mrs. Johnson and arrange for in-school study, for the day of the trip?”

“No,” I said.

“I don’t mind, if it would be easier for you.”

“No.” I shook my head without lifting my eyes from my hard-pointed toes. “I’ll take care of it.”

“I’m so proud of you, CJ. Not every kid could handle all this. But that’s why you’re my superstar.”

I curled myself into a ball over my pointed toes.

eight

Mom made me take off my friendship ring before I walked into class. *No jewelry allowed, you know better than that, CJ. Zoe will hold it for you.* Zoe slipped it onto her pinkie and sat down next to my mother. For an hour and a half, while I took class, I didn't think. I forget everything during class. No noise, no thoughts, just the music, adjusting balance at the barre *a-yum-ba-bi-bum* says the teacher and my body is my whole self. Such a relief. But after, on the ride home, I felt so guilty for dragging Zoe with me all afternoon and then not even quitting, I didn't know what to do. So I made her take off her sneakers and compare toes, to include her. Her toes are a straight line, it turned out; the ideal for going on *pointe,* much better than mine or Morgan's or even Fiona's, whose are pretty good. Zoe was happy about that, I think. I hope it made up to her a little for my not quitting.

Anyway, that was yesterday. Today in school all anybody was talking about was apple picking and soccer. Morgan and Olivia ate lunch together again, whispering. Morgan barely even thanked Zoe for bringing in cleats for her — just grabbed them and dumped them in her locker.

I had to run out of gym class while everybody else was changing out of gym uniforms and into cleats. "'Bye," Zoe said, without looking up at me.

On the way out to Lenox, I told Mom that every one of my friends was at that moment starting soccer.

"Oh, that's exciting," she said. "How are things going with Morgan?"

"Fine."

"So everything worked out."

"I guess."

"I'm so glad," Mom said. "Were you able to arrange things for Monday?"

"Yeah," I lied. It just slipped out.

"What did you arrange?"

I was furious, suddenly. She hadn't even let me talk about soccer. "I'm sitting outside the office doing busy-work all day, OK? While every person in my grade goes to have fun. OK?"

"OK," Mom said softly. "It's hard, I know."

I mumbled, "It's impossible." I pictured myself sitting outside the principal's office, all the little sixth graders walking by wondering if I had in-school suspension, whispering about me, pitying me. How awful. I hated my mother for making me arrange what I hadn't actually arranged, yet.

"So," she began again, "what do you think Yuri will say about your new toe shoes?"

"I don't know." I rested my feet on the front dash, not changing yet.

"I bet he'll be impressed with your feet. I think all the work you did over the summer, strengthening your feet with the exercise bands, is really paying off."

"Thanks," I mumbled. "But I'd rather have cleats."

She laughed, like it was funny.

In class, Yuri said, "Fine, beautiful."

Fiona asked me if I sew in my own ribbons or my mom helps me. She's so competitive. It's what Morgan hated about her when she took ballet, too. "Myself," I told her, limbering up with *grands battements*. "Fiona? Did you ever have to miss a school trip for ballet?"

"Yes."

"Were you furious?"

Fiona shrugged her bony shoulders and held her chin up. "I didn't really care. Only ballet is important to me."

I took my position at the barre.

Tonight, Mom stood over me, watching me sew in my ribbons, showing me where I needed to fold down the back of the shoe a little smoother. Finally I had to let her do the other one. She was so excited, after, she wanted me to try them on for Paul and Daddy, who were at the other end of the dining room table working on Paul's oral report on the five senses. They both looked up to see my toe shoes, but I was like, "Mom!"

"What?" She got out the camera from its cabinet in the front hall. "They're so beautiful, how can you not?"

"I have to call Zoe."

"Just try them on for one minute," she begged. "I love looking at you in them."

I yelled, "Leave me alone!" and stomped up to my room.

My feet were tired — Tuesdays I have regular class plus *pointe* — but after I slammed my door and flopped down on my bed for a few minutes I couldn't help pulling on my new toe shoes and tying the satin ribbons around my ankles. They are so beautiful. I held onto the doorknob to watch myself roll up onto *pointe* in my mirror. Push. Get vertical.

Call Zoe.

I held my doorknob to balance. "How did soccer go?"

I asked Zoe, doing some little *pas de bourrée* in front of the mirror, admiring my feet.

"Good, I guess," she answered. "So, how are the toe shoes?"

"He said they're fine. I'm wearing them right now," I said. "They kill." My feet have gotten stronger, I could see by the way they pulled the shoe into a perfect arch like I couldn't, last year. *Clock-clock.* "I wish I had your toes, though."

"I'm so proud," Zoe said. "I thought they were just stumpy."

I laughed. "Yeah, well, they're perfect. I have to get special shoes with a tapered box and a deep vamp."

"Oh," she said. "I don't know what that means, but I'm sure that's good."

I reached down to twist the right one into a better position on my foot. "You just have a wider base to balance on, if all your toes are the same length," I explained.

"Well, I'm so proud," she said again, and then, "Hold on. No!" she shrieked to someone in the background. "No! I'm on the phone!" She laughed and said, "Quit it!"

"What's happening?" I asked. My family was still at the dining room table, silently researching the senses. Zoe's house is a constant party. Mine, if somebody opens the fridge it causes a commotion.

"My sisters," she said.

I smiled; it sounded like she was having such fun. "What?"

"You know the pencil test? Well, you're so flat-chested, but they want to compare chest size, and — No! You guys! Fine, I'll be off in a minute! Anyway . . ."

"Anyway," I said. "How did soccer go?"

"In a minute!" she yelled to her sisters. "It was great. Everybody was there, it was so much fun."

"Really?" I asked.

"I'm sorry, CJ," she said. "I don't mean to make you feel bad, but, seriously. Can't you just tell your mother you need a break? Just say you need to have some time off to be a kid and hang out with your friends."

"I do," I whispered. "It's really true."

"Yeah." Zoe sounded all enthusiastic. "Tell her all your friends are doing soccer. Right? I mean, not just me — Morgan, and Olivia, and you should've seen Roxanne, oh, my God. She crashed into Bernadette, and the two of them fell on the goal, broke the goalpost."

"You're kidding!" I smiled, imagining it. "I can't believe I missed that."

"You would've died," agreed Zoe. "That's the kind of

thing, though, when you said how many times do you get to be a seventh grader? Things like falling on the goalpost won't crack you up when you're old. Right?"

I nodded. "Probably not."

"Your mom is so nice, she'll understand. Maybe if you just tell her."

I grabbed History off my shelf and scrunched down in the corner of my room, between my dresser and the wall, like when I was little. "She won't understand. She'll say I have to think about my career."

"Your career?" Zoe asked. "You're twelve!"

"Exactly," I said.

"Well, but who does she want you to be friends with?" Zoe asked. "Filona?"

"Fiona." I unlaced my toe shoes.

"Whatever. She's a boring bimbo, you said."

I had to smile. "Morgan said that."

"You agreed," Zoe argued. "Anyway, whatever. I'm sure she's nice."

"She's not." I pulled my toe shoes off and didn't look at the ribbons I hadn't sewn in myself. Fiona thinks she's so great.

"I just . . ." Zoe started. I waited. I heard her sigh, then say quietly, "You would've had a really good time today. You really would've had fun."

"I know," I agreed. "They really broke the goalpost?"

"Shattered it."

I laughed. "I wish I could just quit," I whispered, slipping my toe shoes inside each other. "I never laugh in ballet class."

"Probably no ballerinas are as clumsy as Roxanne, is why."

"Partly," I said. "You know, if I'd been talking to Morgan, she would've said if you want to quit, quit."

"Aren't you glad you're talking to me?" Zoe asked.

"Yes," I said, truthfully. I rested my chin on my knees.

"So tell me what to do. Seriously. I mean, how do I say to my mother, great — you spend all your money and time on seven years of lessons for me, you leave Paul with a baby-sitter he hates three afternoons a week and never have Christmas or Thanksgiving because of my schedule, but, you know what? Too bad if you already paid thousands for this season — I changed my mind! I'm blowing it off to play soccer with my friends?"

"Well," Zoe said. "That might not be the most convincing way to put it."

"I keep thinking of all you guys out there on the lower field having so much fun but then every time I'm about to tell her I quit, I just, I can't figure out any way to make sense."

"Yeah," Zoe said. "Forget it. It doesn't make sense. It would just be that much more fun if you played, too. I'm selfish. You're my best friend. But, I mean, you're totally right."

"I guess." Part of me was really hoping she'd come up with a way of looking at it differently. I snuggled my face into History's fur.

"Also," she whispered. "It's also not just your mom and how giving she is to you. I mean, I saw you last year in *The Nutcracker.* If I could do that . . ."

"What?" I remembered my choreography with my feet, *a-lum-ah-dah.*

"All that, twirling and graceful stuff," Zoe said softly.

I laughed. "I do like the twirling stuff."

"No, I really have a lot of respect for you doing it. I do."

"Thanks," I said. It felt good, that she understood that part of the problem was how great ballet is, too.

"I mean it," Zoe insisted. "So don't listen to me."

"Yeah." I stood up and stuck History up on the shelf where he belonged, then went to flop down on my bed, depressed. "It would be so good, though, being on the team with all you guys."

"Ahh, you're not that great a player anyway."

"Thanks a lot." She's the only person who can make you feel better by insults. "It was really fun?"

"Yeah."

"Ouch." I felt so lonely. "Tell me what else. Tell me everything."

"Well," Zoe said, "the funniest thing was, my mom forgot to pick me up, after."

"She what? What do you mean, forgot to pick you up? What did you do?"

"I just sat there, waiting," Zoe said matter-of-factly. "I mean, I knew they'd realize eventually, so I didn't care or anything. She felt bad when she finally came."

I sat up. "How long were you sitting there?"

"I don't know," she said. "It got dark. But Roxanne waited with me, since she had her bike, so it was fine."

"Oh, Zoe."

"It was pretty funny, actually."

"Funny?" It didn't sound the slightest bit funny to me.

"Yeah," she insisted. "My family was all sitting down

to dinner, and everybody was like, where's Zoe, where's Zoe, and I guess then my mother was like, oops!"

I didn't know what to say to her. My mother would never forget me. When soccer started last year, my mother shadowed me up and down the field on the sidelines yelling, *Don't run, CJ!*

"Do you want me to come over?" I asked Zoe. It was dark out already, and I was supposed to be rinsing my new maroon leotard, doing my homework, and getting ready for bed, but I felt like Zoe might really need me, after something like that. Mom would understand and drive me over, if I explained to her what happened to Zoe today. I wandered over to my desk and sat down in my desk chair to put on socks and my sneakers.

"You want to come over now?" Zoe asked.

"My mom will drive me over, I'm sure," I said, but right away slapped myself on the head — what am I, an idiot? What, like it will make Zoe feel better for me to tell her how understanding my mother is? "If . . ." I tried to think quick what to say, but I really am not a very quick thinker. "Are you, I mean, depressed?" I rolled my eyes at myself in the mirror.

"No," Zoe said. "You mean about my mom?"

"Yeah." I shook my head. All I want to do is be nice, and I end up such a jerk.

"It was funny," Zoe said again, sounding less sure. "I don't care."

"OK." How would I feel, I wondered, if Mom ever really did leave me alone? I tried to think what in the world to say. "Anyway."

"Anyway," she repeated. "Has Tommy called you?"

"No." I flopped back onto my bed. "Hey, did you think about Lou?"

"Lou?" she asked.

"If you like him."

"Are you serious?" I couldn't tell if she was laughing or angry.

"Don't you think it would be fun?" I asked, taking my time with the words. "He's good friends with Tommy and . . ."

"I like him," Zoe protested. "He's my buddy, he draws funny comics even if they're all about battles in World War Two. I have nothing against the guy, but he's a, sort of, a doof, don't you think?"

I pulled the big blue sweatshirt Zoe had given me last week out of the closet and held it in front of myself, in the mirror. “He’s nice. I think he likes you. I saw him looking at you, today.”

“Ew. No. Really? When?”

I smiled. She sounded a little interested. “At lunch.”

“I bring big sandwiches,” she said. “He probably just thinks I’m fat.”

“He does not!” She tries to seem like she doesn’t care, but I know she does. I pulled the sweatshirt over my head and dropped the phone. “Sorry,” I said when I got it back up to my ear. “I was putting on your sweatshirt. Bluie.”

“Big Blue,” she said softly, so I couldn’t really hear her.

“What?”

“Big Blue,” she repeated, loud.

“Oh, yeah. Big Blue. It’s so soft.”

“I know,” she said.

I decided to change the subject again. "Anyway, what were you saying?"

"Nothing," she mumbled. "Just, you know. Boys don't like me that way."

"That's not true." She heard Morgan say that about her last week. Morgan has said that a lot. Maybe it is true, maybe not — but Lou might. He seems more mature than the rest of the boys. I couldn't think what else to say to make Zoe feel better. Everything I was trying seemed to backfire. I decided not to say anything.

"Anyway," she said, after a while of silence. "You do the math yet?"

"Yeah."

"Me, too," she said. "So . . ."

I waited another while and then asked, "Zoe? I, if you,

I think he really does like you, Lou. And if, do you, I could, you want me to ask Tommy for you?"

"No," she said. She said it really almost angrily. I never heard her sound angry before.

"OK," I said quietly.

"I mean, let me think about it. OK?"

"OK." I took off my sneakers and my socks. "Are you mad at me?"

"No," she said.

I curled up on my bed with History and picked at the seam in my wallpaper. It has little rosebuds. Mom had chosen it when I was little because, she said, it was so "me."

"OK! OK!" Zoe yelled at her sisters. "I gotta go, they need my body. See you tomorrow!"

"OK," I said, hanging up.

Why can't I be fun? I asked History. He just looked at me blankly. *Who does she want me to be friends with?* I stood up and got the permission slip out of my book bag. No matter how many times I reread it, it still said we'd get back at six-thirty, just as I'd be pulling off my ballet slippers and yanking my dance pants over my tights for the long ride home alone with my mother.

nine

I have never felt so alone as I felt today.

Just about every girl in the entire school was wearing a soccer shirt. I was sitting up on the wall this morning before school, watching purple jersey after purple jersey come toward me like waves. Purple jerseys with huge black-and-white soccer balls on the fronts. Nobody said anything about it to me; in fact, nobody really looked at me. Worst of all, I chose today to wear my pale-yellow minidress. Zoe and Roxanne were comparing game schedules, Morgan and Olivia sat on the ground below the wall, whispering as usual. All in their purple jerseys.

I didn't even go to my locker when the bell rang; I went straight to homeroom in hopes of avoiding all the excitement. Nobody seemed to notice.

"Hi, CJ," Ms. Cress said.

"Hi." I crossed my arms on my desk and rested my head on top.

She came over and sat on the desk next to mine. "We missed you at soccer yesterday."

I didn't answer.

"You're not playing this year?"

"I have ballet," I said. "Four times a week."

"Wow. 'K. We'll miss you."

I wanted to cry. "Thanks."

"Did you bring in your permission slip for apple picking?"

"No," I mumbled into my arms. "I forgot it."

"What am I gonna do with you?" She shook me. "Bring it in tomorrow, 'K? I really want to win the cookie. It's huge, and you know I hate to lose. Especially to Ms. Masters."

"'K," I said, still not looking up.

I didn't lift my head all through homeroom and took the long way to Spanish. When I got there, Morgan and Olivia were already inside, their heads close to each other's. Morgan used to lean close to *me* when she talked.

"Hey," Tommy said.

I turned around and almost bumped into him. I dropped my lunch. An orange rolled out of it down the hall, and while I picked up my sandwich, Tommy ran after my orange. "You're not on soccer?" he asked, handing it to me.

I shrugged. "Dance."

"So?"

"So I can't do both! OK?"

"OK, OK," he said. "I just wanted to ask you . . ."

Gideon bumped him, going in to Spanish, and coughed "hay-stacking" into his hands.

"Shut up," Tommy said. He rested the heel of one untied high-top on top of his other foot.

I waited. The bell rang.

I started heading in to class, but Tommy licked his bottom lip and whispered, "Will you sit with me on the bus to apple picking?"

"Sure," I said.

All through Spanish I was like, *What? I couldn't believe I said yes, but it was like, how could I say no — he finally talked to me and it was to ask me to sit with him. I had to say yes.* When I looked at him just before our vocab quiz, he smiled a little, just enough to show his deep dimples. I could barely hold my pen. None of the vocab words sounded the slightest bit familiar. How do you say, "My boyfriend"?

He waited for me in the doorway after Spanish. We started walking together toward Ms. Cress's room. My arm brushed against his, which felt very warm. "Sorry," I said. I was shaking.

"That's OK," he answered. We kept walking, looking straight ahead. I could feel other kids looking at us. "Hot today, huh?" he asked.

"Yeah," I agreed, and we kept walking. I checked my bun. It was holding fine. I watched our feet moving together in unison, though his were clomping in his untied high-tops. I tried to think of anything in the world to say to him.

We passed a poster in the hall announcing the Seventh-Grade Unity Trip, and he rolled his eyes. "They think a couple of slogans will make us act nice to one another."

"Yeah," I agreed. I didn't know what else to say. He and Zoe always tease each other, banter back and forth. I kept nodding, trying to think of something witty, something Zoe might say. Which reminded me. I asked, "You know Lou?"

He looked at me out of the corner of his eyes. "Uh, yeah," he said. Of course he knows Lou.

"Does he like Zoe?" I asked.

Tommy squinted his eyes at me like he was trying to understand. "*Like* her, like her?"

"Yeah." I checked my bun again. Still holding.

"Why? Does she like Lou?"

"Just find out," I whispered. "OK?"

He shrugged and sped up. I felt somebody staring at me so I turned around. Morgan was right behind me, shaking her head.

I walked faster. When I got to math, Zoe was already there. She smiled at me, and even though she was wearing a soccer jersey like everybody else, at least she looked happy to see me. I went right over to her. "I asked Tommy for you," I whispered.

"What?"

I felt my insides all clench. I blinked a few times. "You don't have to, I just, to find out, I didn't say you liked him or anything. . . ."

Zoe looked all pale. She slumped down into her seat.

"What happened?" Olivia asked.

"Nothing," I insisted. I looked up at the front of the classroom where Tommy and Lou were talking. I guess Zoe looked up at the same time, because she clonked her head down onto her desk.

Morgan came over and leaned on my desk. "You think you're so special, don't you?" she whispered.

I shook my head. "What?"

"What happened?" Olivia asked again.

"Nothing!" I sank into my seat.

"She's fixing up Zoe with Lou," Morgan said. "Do you even like Lou?" she asked Zoe.

Without raising her face off the desk, Zoe shook her head.

The bell rang, and Ms. Cress asked everybody to take their seats.

Morgan leaned close to me but didn't smile. "Not everybody needs a boyfriend," she whispered.

"I didn't say . . ."

"You just think you're so great to have a boyfriend and be a little ballerina, in your ballerina dress, so much better than the rest of us."

"I do-do-do-do not." I could feel myself starting to cry. Zoe wouldn't pick her head up. Olivia, when I looked at her, bowed her head. I guess she agreed, too. Morgan was whispering, but it felt like the whole room was listening to her and agreeing.

"You go ahead," Morgan whispered. "Do everything you can to set yourself apart. I hope you're impressed with yourself, superstar. The rest of us will be perfectly happy to stick together in the shadows."

ten

Nobody talked much to me the rest of the day. I told Zoe I had to go to the library during lunch because I'd been too tired to do my social studies homework after ballet. She said OK. Maybe she was relieved. In English/social studies, I passed a note to Tommy saying, *Never mind about Lou*. He shrugged. I told everybody at our lockers, between seventh and eighth, that I'd told Tommy to forget it about Lou and Zoe. They all said things like, "Whatever."

I walked all the way to band alone and sat there behind my music pretending to play, my flute resting against my quivering lip. By the time the final bell rang, my flute was in pieces in the case in my bag. I was out the front door of school by the time Mom pulled into the circle.

Mom asked me what was wrong, but I didn't tell her. She turned on the radio. I turned it off. She left it off. I spent the whole afternoon in my room, because Wednesdays I have nothing. She was at Cub Scouts with Paul, anyway. And all my friends had soccer.

When I got to school this morning, I didn't sit on the wall. I passed Morgan and walked straight to Ms. Cress's classroom, but I didn't go in right away. I looked at the board through the glass panel next to the door. Mine was the last name left on the board, the only one who hadn't brought in her permission slip for apple picking. On top of everything else, it was my fault Ms. Cress would lose the cookie. *Cornelia Jane Hurley,* right up there on the board for the whole world to see. I hate my name so much.

I managed to get through the day without crying, without talking, without being a show-off or acting special in any way — until eighth period.

The gym was all set up for gymnastics. Rings hung down from the ceiling and so did three ropes. Red and blue mats were pushed together in the corner near the fire exit. A balance beam slanted away from the bleachers where we sat, waiting to be divided into teams by Mr. Brock, the gym teacher, who is supposedly going out with Ms. Cress. It's the scandal.

I was a Two, Zoe was a Three. Morgan takes chorus instead of band, so she has gym opposite days of us. I was relieved to be away from her. Zoe had eaten lunch with me and said it was no big deal, as long as I told

Tommy forget it, it's history. I kept apologizing. She said don't worry, but it's hard to tell if she means it.

I wandered over to the beam with the other Twos. If you annoy Mr. Brock, you go down for push-ups until he blows his whistle. If you do push-ups you develop big biceps. Swans have long, skinny, graceful arms. I always keep my mouth shut and my head down in gym, then race out afterward to my mother's waiting car. The best part about being in gym class is everybody wears a white T-shirt and blue shorts, including me. I blend in.

Tommy was a Two, too. We stood next to each other, waiting our turn, staring at our sneakers as the first Two crossed the beam. "Hi," Tommy whispered.

"Hi," I whispered back. I pressed the tops of my toes against the floor to stretch my arch and tried to think of something witty to say. I'm so bad at that. So we just stood there, me thinking, *My boyfriend! Say something!* And him thinking . . . I have no idea what.

I said, "Oh," about to tell him I couldn't sit with him on the apple-picking trip, when Mr. Brock said, "Tommy? If you're done flirting, cross the beam."

Tommy mounted the beam exactly the way Mr. Brock taught us last week, held his hands out and wobbled as he stood up, but then walked quickly across.

"Stop," barked Mr. Brock.

Tommy stopped, tottered, and fell off down to the mat. I gasped.

"Get up," Mr. Brock said.

Tommy stood up. He was blushing, and his skinny, tan legs were shaking. He didn't look back at the rest of us Twos as he placed his hands on the beam and hoisted himself up again.

"I want to see some grace, this time," Mr. Brock demanded.

Tommy walked slower this time to the end of the beam and jumped off. Roxanne clapped for him, then immediately got down into push-up position.

"Give me fifty," said Mr. Brock.

Tommy walked over, stood next to me again, and asked, "Are you gonna say the pledge?"

I realized my hand was over my heart, like Mom when she's nervous. I dropped my hand and looked down at Roxanne. She was blowing a kiss at Mr. Brock's back, from down on the mat. Roxanne doesn't care what anybody thinks. She drops her books constantly and holds her belly when she laughs and chews with her mouth open. I think she's probably smarter than Ken Carpenter or Olivia, but she's too busy getting in trouble to copy over her work, the way teachers like, so she doesn't get the same kind of credit as they do. I like her, though, even though probably she thinks I'm boring.

I smiled at her.

"Twinkle Toes," Mr. Brock said to me. I looked at my sneakers. It's hard to imagine that Ms. Cress is really going out with him. She's so cool and he's so mean. He's cute, I guess, in a broad-shouldered, scrubbed way — that must be what Ms. Cress likes.

"Sorry," I mumbled.

"Since we have a real ballerina here," Mr. Brock said, "let's all watch how she does the balance beam." He blew his whistle. Roxanne stopped pretending to do push-ups. Mr. Brock blew his whistle again. "Everyone, gather 'round." He crossed his arms across his muscular chest. I looked at the big clock up high on the wall — only eight minutes until the bell and I could change out of this stupid white T-shirt and crappy blue shorts and run out to the circle where Mom is probably already waiting to drive me to dance, since I haven't managed to quit. Eight minutes. Seven. I wished for Mr. Brock to forget about me and choose somebody else.

"Up you go," he said to me. He really meant it. I bent my feet against the floor and watched them, one after the other, forming graceful capital C's. My feet are getting stronger, I told myself — I can bring the sole of my sneaker along with the arch of my foot, which I never used to be able to manage. Too bad Tommy wouldn't know how cool that is.

Kids jumped off the rings and slid down the ropes. "We're all waiting," Mr. Brock told me. Seven minutes until the bell. Everybody in the middle school who takes band is in this gym class, and they were all crunching together on the yellow mats beside the beam.

"Please," I whispered to Mr. Brock. "I'm sorry." If my mother knew I was about to climb up on the beam, she'd have an absolute fit. You could do a lot worse than just twist an ankle, falling from up there.

"I want you people to see how the balance beam is done," announced Mr. Brock. "CJ?"

"I don't, I d-d-d . . ."

"I don't, I don't, I don't," he said back.

I placed my hands on the beam like Tommy had and got myself up to a standing position. My feet were beside Mr. Brock's whistle. He has a bald spot at the top of his blond head I'd never seen before. It made him seem less tough and gorgeous, more like my dad. *Imagine he's Dad,*

I told myself. *Just do whatever he says and it'll be over, you won't have to talk.*

"Do some ballerina tricks or something," he suggested, crossing his arms.

I felt myself wobbling. "I don't, we, there's no b-b-b-balance beam . . ." I stuttered. *Don't fall,* I warned myself.

"I don't, I don't, I don't," he said.

I gripped myself tighter, in a hug. *Whatever you do, don't fall.*

"We'll all just stand here and wait," Mr. Brock told me. "I got no place to go until seven o'clock tonight."

Hate.

Kids below me shuffled their feet and sighed. I couldn't budge. The bell rang, and a few kids started breaking for the gym door, but Mr. Brock barked, "Not until I say dismissed."

Everybody looked back up at me.

"Come on, ballerina."

I was breathing through my mouth, looking up at the ceiling, praying not to cry.

"An arabesque," I heard Zoe yell.

I couldn't risk falling off to turn and ask if she'd lost her mind, helping the gym teacher humiliate me, when she's supposed to be my best friend. *Forget it,* I thought, *I'm taking off this ring.* Morgan would never have yelled an arabesque. Probably Zoe was getting back at me about Lou.

"Yeah," said Mr. Brock. "An arabesque!"

It'll end, I told myself. *Do it and be done,* I told myself. *You have no choice,* I told myself.

My arms ungripped my T-shirt and dropped to my sides, then lifted softly to *port de bras.* My body tilted slightly forward, adjusting the balance, and I relaxed into dance class mode. *Square the chest, and leg up, higher, higher, and, stay. Balance. Ahh. Toes, toes, toes — point hard, extend the line. Don't move. Chin up, chin up, long neck. Breathe. Position, hold. No thoughts.*

Then I crouched down and jumped off the beam. Mr. Brock yelled dismissed, but I was already pushing open the door to the girls' locker room.

"What a jerk," Zoe whispered, right behind me.

"Mmm-hmm." I didn't want to open my mouth and risk crying.

"Are you mad at me?" Zoe asked. "I just said that because, I tried to think how to get you down from there."

I sniffed. She had a point.

"That was so unfair of him," she whispered, "singling you out like that."

In front of our gym lockers, I yanked off my T-shirt and shorts, not even caring if she or anybody saw my flat body. "I'm so sick of—"

"Of what?" Zoe asked.

"Do you think, seriously"—I looked in her eyes—"do I try to act special?"

Zoe shrugged. "You are special."

"You sound like my mother." I jumped to yank my jeans over both feet at once.

"Sorry," Zoe said. She wiggled into her soccer shirt.

"Do I, though?" I whispered. "What Morgan said yesterday. Do I act all, better, separate from everybody?"

Zoe sat down. She didn't answer or look up as she strapped her shin guards onto her legs and pulled her long soccer socks over them.

"I don't want to be," I said, pulling my book bag out of the gym locker. It got caught on the part of the locker that sticks out to catch the door. It frustrated me so much I just tugged and tugged until it tore free, making a little rip in the front of it. I slammed the bag down on the bench. "I just . . ." I was so angry — at Mom, at Mr. Brock, at Tommy — everybody who makes me feel like a stupid little jerk separate from the whole world. "That's not what I want to be," I said.

"What?" Zoe wiggled her foot into a cleat, then looked up.

"Separate."

Mom, I'm sure, was craning her neck trying to hurry me up. I sat down on the bench. I unzipped my ripped bag and pulled out my blue folder. I opened the folder and pulled out the permission slip, then dug around in the bottom of my bag for a pen. I spread the permission slip carefully on the bench, read it over, and signed my mother's name.

"I'm going apple picking," I said.

"Are you sure?" Zoe asked. She tied her cleats in double bows while she looked over what I had done.

I smiled. "I have to do what's right for me."

"True," said Zoe. "But what if you get caught? I mean, you're, you'll, you —"

"Breathe," I told her. I felt so calm, it was weird.

She took a breath and asked, "What's gonna happen?"

"It will all work out."

"Are you sure?"

I nodded. "I have every confidence."

eleven

I handed my permission slip to Ms. Cress in homeroom the next morning.

"Finally!" she said. "But Ms. Masters won the cookie."

"Sorry."

She shrugged. "Sometimes you win, usually you lose."

"Oh," I said. "And I was, is it, I mean, can I still get on the soccer team?"

"I thought ballet interfered."

"No," I said. "We just decided it was too much, ballet four times a week. It didn't leave time for anything else."

Ms. Cress nodded. "It did seem like a lot."

“Mmm-hmm,” I said. “So I’ll just, take ballet Fridays, because we don’t have soccer Fridays, right?”

“Right,” she said.

I smiled, surprised by how calm I felt. I’d had this weird, foggy, relaxed feeling from the moment I forged my mother’s signature on my permission slip. All through dance class yesterday I felt it, and ironically I danced better than ever — even Fiona complimented me. At dinner, Paul told us about giving his oral report on the four senses — he totally forgot the sense of taste. He was really funny; we all laughed until our eyes were watering. Daddy came in to give me a special kiss later when I was in bed and told me he was glad I was feeling back to normal. He hadn’t kissed me in a while.

“Great!” Ms. Cress said, going to her desk. “So you can start Tuesday.”

I nodded. "Yeah. After the trip."

"I saved number five, just in case," she said.

"Really?"

"Well, not too many of the girls would fit into such a small shirt, anyway," she admitted.

"My lucky number," I said. "It's all working out."

"Where are those forms?" Ms. Cress asked herself, riffling through the mess on her desk. "I know they're here somewhere. I'm happy you'll play, CJ. We can always use a player who has your, your . . ." She was searching not just for the forms, I knew, but for an adjective to describe my lousy soccer abilities in a nice way. "Here. With your enthusiasm," she finally said, holding a packet of forms in the air triumphantly.

"It's OK," I said. "I know I stink. I just, I like, I-I-I want to, like to be a part of the team."

"Great attitude." She laid the forms on my desk, placed her hand on my shoulder, and bent over to show me. "This one is the schedule, this yellow is the medical form, the pink is the parental release form — try to be quicker with that one?"

"Ha," I sort of laughed.

"And this blue one, oh! That's for ordering your soccer jacket. It's optional, and it's forty-nine dollars, so talk it over with your parents. 'K?"

"I'm sure they'll say yes," I told her. "They're very supportive of-of-of soccer. Playing. And, jackets. They really want me to be on the team, so . . ."

Shut up, I told myself.

"Good to have you on the team," she said. "Come to the gym at lunch, if you want to pick up your team jersey."

"I do," I told her.

twelve

I walked into the cafeteria, straight over to the table where all my friends were sitting, and pulled my new soccer shirt out of my bag. Everybody's eyes opened wide. I just smiled.

"But . . ." said Olivia.

"You . . ." said Morgan.

I climbed onto the bench and sat down across from Zoe, who kept blinking. I shrugged, opened my lunch bag, and looked in. "I just decided I'd rather be on the soccer team," I said slowly, taking my time with the words I'd rehearsed in my head the whole way over from the gym.

"Rather than what?" Olivia asked.

"Rather than dance."

"You're quitting dance?"

"No need to alert the media," I told her. That's Tommy's favorite expression. I saw Zoe smile a tiny bit, just the corners of her mouth. "Or your mother," I added, realizing too late that Olivia would probably tell her mother as soon as she got home, and Aunt Betsy would call my mother, and I'd be caught.

I tried to remain calm.

Olivia blushed. "Well, what did you mother say?" she asked. "She must be devastated."

Olivia always says stuff like *devastated* when a normal person would say *mad.* I knew I was furious at Olivia mainly because she had the power to ruin everything for me, but still. I shrugged again. "It's my decision."

"When did you realize that?" Morgan asked.

"Yesterday," I said.

Morgan smiled but quickly blew her bangs out of her eyes to cover it up.

"She's disappointed, of course," I added, trying to imagine the ideal scene between me and Mom. "She said she wished I felt differently, but that I have to do what's right for me."

I looked at Zoe, who took a huge bite of her sandwich. She's the only one who knew I was making this all up. I pulled out my yogurt and took a spoonful.

"Well," said Olivia. "Congratulations."

"Thanks. And I'm coming apple picking, too."

Morgan looked up from her lunch. Last year when those kids got caught hay-stacking, we spent lots of afternoons imagining what it would be like when we were finally in seventh grade, and who we'd want to hay-stack with, and promising that even if we had boyfriends we'd tell them sorry, I'm sitting with my best friend. She was planning Tommy for herself and Jonas for me, then.

Olivia unwrapped her box of pretzel sticks and offered some to me. For the first time ever, I accepted. "I was wondering why your name was finally erased from Ms. Cress's board," she said.

"That's why." I chewed. The pretzel sticks tasted great.

"I guess we won't be having a class trip to see you in *The Nutcracker* this year, then," Morgan pointed out.

I took a deep breath and didn't answer. I tried to smile like, so what? I don't care about that. The *Nutcracker* music from the entrance of the Polichinelles blared in my head.

Morgan crumpled her lunch bag and tossed it over me into the garbage can. We all watched it arch in perfectly. She leaned toward Olivia and asked, "You ready to go outside?"

Olivia chewed faster, swallowed, and said, "Yeah."

After they both left, I stopped smiling and leaned toward Zoe. "I'm so caught."

"I know," Zoe whispered back and stood up. "Let's go talk."

"What am I going to do?" I asked Zoe on the way, trying to block out the *Nutcracker* music inside me. "No way Olivia won't tell her mother."

"Shhh," Zoe said. "Wait till we're safe."

When we got into the girls' room she checked under the stalls — no feet. "OK," she said.

I smiled.

"What?"

"Nothing." I shook my head. "I feel like we're in a movie, checking under the stalls like that."

Zoe laughed, then whispered, "The nuclear weapons are in the black attaché case."

Roxanne came in, so we both shut up. She went straight into a stall. When she came out and was washing her hands, she looked back at me in the mirror. "You quit dance?"

"Wow. News travels fast," I said.

She tore a paper towel out of the dispenser, dried her hands, and started to leave. "Can I get the social studies from you, Zoe?" she asked.

"Sure," Zoe said. "Be out in a few."

"Thanks." The door banged Roxanne in the behind as

she left. We could hear her say "Ow," in the hall, and we smiled at each other.

"You're so nice," I told Zoe. "No wonder everybody likes you."

"Please," Zoe said.

"What? You were sixth-grade president. And fifth." I was nominated last year for sixth-grade secretary but I lost. My parents helped me make posters with white marker on black oak tag. They were unique, and my dad's printing is excellent because he's an architect, but, well, no big deal. Secretary is a lousy job anyway.

"Yeah, well," Zoe said. "Giving out your homework always helps."

I shrugged and smiled, but then covered my face with

my hands, breathed twice, then looked up at her. "Olivia's mother and mine talk every day."

"Yikes."

"Well," I said, trying to be confident, the new me. "I'll just have to keep my mother from talking to her."

"All weekend?"

"At least until I explain."

"You're gonna tell her you forged your permission slip?" Zoe's eyes opened huge.

"I haven't actually come up with a plan yet," I admitted. "I just feel like, something will come to me. You know? Something will happen, and I'll tell her, and it'll be fine."

Zoe shook her head without taking her big blue eyes off me. "OK," she said. "Sounds good to me."

"Can you sleep over Saturday?" I asked her.

"I thought you were sleeping over my house."

I shook my head. "I have to sit by the phone all weekend. Right? Well, actually, except Olivia's mother volunteers at the science museum Saturdays until three. So we could still go pay our installment on the rings then. I'll be done with dance and home by noon, and my mom could pick you up and drop us off at Sundries and then pick us up at three. OK?"

"Um, OK," Zoe said. "Whew, complicated."

"And then we could do whatever at my house on Saturday and be there in case the phone rings and grab it so Olivia's mother doesn't have a chance to tell my mom. And also, in case I figure out a way to tell her, you'll be there, so she can't get too furious at me."

"OK," Zoe said again, blinking a lot. "Wow, talk about being in the movies. You should be a spy."

I smiled at her. "Thanks," I said. "I'm sorry about the whole Lou thing."

"Forget it already," Zoe said. "Come on. I have to go cheat with Roxanne."

thirteen

The way to tell my mother didn't come to me Friday night. I was so busy trying to make sure she didn't call Aunt Betsy, I didn't really get much chance to think. While we were eating dinner, Mom said, "Oh, I have to call Betsy and see how Olivia did today."

"At what?" I asked, in my best imitation of a calm voice.

"Her braces."

I had totally forgotten that Olivia was getting her braces put on after school.

"Was she nervous at school today?" Mom asked me, passing the string beans to Paul, who took one.

"Yes, a little," I guessed. "But she said the whole family was planning to pick her up and go out for frozen yogurt for dinner and then, um, a movie. So, they won't get home until very late. You know," I added, "to take her mind off it."

I waited to see how they would react. Before this year I never even lied about if I'd brushed my teeth. Mom and Dad looked at each other. "Isn't that nice," Dad said.

Mom nodded and passed Paul the potatoes. I felt myself smiling — such a powerful thing, lying. Before, I always thought they'd just know if I made something up — like they'd be able to tell, like there was no privacy inside my own head. But, there is.

I swallowed my mashed potatoes and asked, "Can Zoe sleep over here, tomorrow, instead of me going there?"

"Sure, of course," Mom answered. "Why?"

"She just really likes it here," I invented. May as well make them feel good. I was feeling powerful enough to be generous.

"I'm glad," Mom said. "Maybe you and Zoe could baby-sit for Paul, then, and Dad and I could go out?"

They smiled at each other.

"I don't need a baby-sitter," Paul said.

"You're eight," reminded Dad.

"But I'm very mature."

"We'd be happy to," I answered generously. It would be good to get Mom out of the house and away from the possibility of hearing my news from Aunt Betsy —

worth having to pay attention to Paul. "Zoe likes Paul, too." Why not? Zoe likes everybody. I think Paul blushed. "We'll do fun stuff," I told him. "I promise."

I was up this morning before Mom woke me, but I pretended to be asleep. She reminded me to use the exercise bands for my feet at the end of my stretching. I did an extra five on each foot, promising myself that on the way to dance, I'd tell Mom everything.

But I didn't. Where to start? She'd be so disappointed in everything I'd done — forging, quitting, backing out of my commitment, lying. . . . I decided I'd wait until after class. Another few hours of having her like me and trust me. As Zoe had said, "The longer you can avoid a conflict, the better."

Class was good, again. I wasn't falling out of my turns. Sometimes dance class is even better than performing, because it's like an hour and a half away from thinking anything. Your body works, your mind is in quiet mode. No words, just the teacher counting out beats: *la, yum, ba-bi-bum.* Position! And when you're on, when you're focused and pushing, higher on the jumps — straighter legs — longer line — hold! Ah. Yes. There's nothing else but the clacking of toe shoes or the whispering of ballet slippers against the wood floor, the plonking of the piano, and your fingers brushing the barre.

When Yuri clapped to signal the end of class, I looked up at the clock, surprised it had gone so fast. Next to me, Fiona bent to pull her black sweater pants over her tights. "Strong work today," she said, the second time in a row.

"Thanks. You, too." I hadn't noticed her but she's always good.

She put on her thin, flowered tank-sweatshirt and strode toward the door. "See you Monday," she called.

"Monday," I echoed. "Oh . . ."

"What?" She stopped and turned around. She is so bony even her eyes bulge out.

I felt like I should tell her, *No, I won't see you Monday because I'll be apple picking,* but instead I said, "Nothing. I just, nothing."

She stretched her neck, then left. It's often between me and Fiona for parts in recitals or now, ballets. I wondered if she would miss my company in class or be happy to be rid of the competition. It's different with ballet friends. There's always an edge, and you don't tell each other your secrets, you just don't. I think we're too used to standing silently close in class and in the wings to figure out how to chatter together.

Mom and I walked out to the car, and she started the engine before she told me she had peeked in and seen me, and that she was impressed with my focus. "Your dancing is really blossoming," she said. "I'm so excited for you. I think this year will be a real jump forward, professionally, for you."

I couldn't very well tell her I was quitting after that, so I just changed my clothes and didn't talk, all the way to Zoe's house. Aunt Betsy wouldn't be around until after three anyway, so I had a little leeway.

Zoe was waiting for us on her front lawn, wearing cut-off shorts and a red sweatshirt. She waved as we pulled into her driveway. I had put on the old blue sweatshirt she'd lent me and my short yellow shorts, so we were dressed similarly, which made me happy. I never cared about stuff like that until recently, but I guess since

Wednesday, especially, I keep stressing about being the only one wearing the wrong thing.

I unbuckled my seat belt and turned around to smile at Zoe in the backseat. "Hi!"

"Hi." She raised her eyebrows. I shook my head. She shrugged. We can talk like that, have a whole conversation with no words. It's so incredible. It feels like we were really meant to be best friends. I turned back around and buckled up as Mom pulled out into the street.

Just before we got to town, Mom started steering with her knee so she could pull out her wallet to give me my allowance.

I grabbed her wallet for her. "Can I get it?"

"Such a worrywart," she said, smiling at Zoe in the rearview mirror.

I took the bills and thanked her, placing the wallet back into her pocketbook.

"You're welcome. So I'll pick you up around four?"

"No!" I panicked. All the calm I had been feeling exploded away. "Three, you said three." Olivia's mother could get home, Mom could call her, and Aunt Betsy would definitely say, *Are you devastated that CJ's quitting dance?* And Mom would be like, *What?* And then I could just see her face when she picked us up — confused, angry, disappointed.

"That's not much time," Mom said.

"It's plenty," I said. I could feel my heart pounding — tell her, tell her! — but I couldn't. The time wasn't right. We had to pay our installment for our friendship rings. "We have, have, h-h-homework. A project. To work on."

"Yeah," Zoe agreed.

I closed my eyes and tried not to have a heart attack.

"OK," Mom said. "OK. See you at four, then."

"Three!" I opened my eyes. We were in front of Sundries, and Mom was smiling.

"Kidding," Mom said.

"It's not funny," I said, getting out. "It's an important project."

"Sorry."

I leaned into the car. "Sorry," I whispered. "Love you."

She blew me a kiss, then peeled out.

I shook my head at Zoe.

She touched her old blue sweatshirt sleeve on my arm and asked, "Tense?"

"Phew, a little."

We walked into Sundries to pay our weekly two dollars each. I was about to head straight for the counter, but a familiar laugh made me look over toward the card section. Morgan and Olivia were there. They looked up and saw us at the same time. We all waved at each other, and Zoe and I walked back there toward them.

Olivia's mouth looked full. "How are the braces?" I asked her.

She smiled, sort of, to show them.

"Wow," Zoe said. Olivia's mouth was really, really packed with silver. "Does it hurt?"

"It killed, getting them on," Olivia said. "And I can't eat anything. I'm starving." She almost drooled, but covered her mouth in time.

We all shook our heads, sympathetically, but then I panicked. "Did your mother drive you guys here?"

"We walked," she said, through her hand.

"Because your mother is at the museum until three, right?"

Olivia just nodded.

I smiled at her, so relieved. "Getting psyched for apple picking?"

"We're buying some candy and stuff," Morgan said.

"Not that I can eat it," mumbled Olivia.

"We'll buy some, too," I offered.

Zoe shrugged. "I'm always up for candy."

"I think it'll be really fun," I said.

"You don't still like Tommy, do you?" Morgan asked me. We all looked at her for a few seconds. Morgan carefully replaced the birthday card she'd been holding in the rack. "After yesterday?"

"What?" Zoe asked.

Morgan looked at Zoe like she was shocked. "You don't know?"

Olivia, Zoe, and I all shook our heads.

"After CJ told Tommy to, you know, forget about it? He was going around the upper playground after school like, Zoe and Lou, Zoe and Lou — he was telling everybody you're after him." She shook her head at Zoe. "I thought you knew."

Zoe swallowed hard. All three of them bowed their heads and looked at me from under their eyebrows.

"I-I-I . . ." I didn't know what to say. After everything, if Zoe starts hating me for this mess, I don't know what I'll do. Run away to my grandmother's farm and live there for the rest of my life, maybe. How bad could cow poop and milk drippings really be?

"It's not your fault," Morgan said to me. "I mean, you shouldn't have said anything to him in the first place, but once you told him to forget it, he didn't have to be such a jerk."

Olivia nodded. She has a very strict sense of morality. "That's just cruel," she said, then made a big slurping sound. "Sorry. It's really hard to control your spit when you first get braces."

"Don't worry about it," Morgan said. "We understand."

Zoe and I nodded. Zoe was still busy inspecting her sneakers, thumping the right one against the dingy gray Sundries carpet.

"Thanks," said Olivia. "See? That's what I mean. Girls are so much nicer than boys."

"He really did that?" Zoe asked Morgan.

"I thought you knew," Morgan said. "That's why I thought, well, I figured CJ probably broke up with him. I would. But, whatever."

"I'm going to," I said.

"Really?" Zoe asked.

I made myself nod. "That's just, I mean, that's so cruel. And you're my, you're more important to me, than, so . . ."

"We have to stick together," Olivia said, slurping again. "Sorry."

"It's OK," I said. "And if the boys think they're getting any of our candy . . ."

"They can suck our shoelaces," Zoe said. We all cracked up.

The four of us went over to the candy aisle and even found some Life Savers, which Olivia thought she could probably handle, in addition to red licorice and a bag of miniature Snickers. Zoe read over the label, which said, SNICKERS FUN SIZE, and said, "Boy, this sure is a fun size!"

"I never had such fun," Morgan said. "Not with any other size!"

"I'm having fun already," I added, but the laughter was dying down a little, and the three of them looked at me sort of quizzically.

"What?" Olivia asked.

"Hey," I said. "I was just thinking, when you said we have to stick together or whatever?" I looked at Morgan, then down at her feet in their clunky sandals. Perfect turn-out.

"What about it?" Morgan asked.

I looked over at Zoe, but I couldn't tell if she agreed with what I was about to do or if she even knew. But she's such a friendly person, I decided she probably would be happy.

"Well," I started, slowly, carefully. "Zoe and I got these rings here last week, and I was thinking, wouldn't it be great if you guys got them, too?"

Zoe blinked a lot of times in a row.

"I don't know," Morgan said, her hands resting on her hips.

"It could be like a th-th-thing," I said. "Like a, you know, like a bond. Between us."

"Among us," Olivia said. "'Between' is if there are only two."

"Whatever," I said. My left eye was twitching, and behind it I could feel my pulse.

"I don't know if Zoe wants us to," Morgan said.

"Me?" Zoe asked. Her smile looked a little nauseated.

"They have plenty. In a bag. Under the thing. Counter. These aren't the only two."

I wanted to suck the offer right back into my mouth.

Morgan and Olivia looked at each other and shrugged.

"Do you want to?" Olivia asked Morgan.

"I don't have much money with me," Morgan said.

"I have, don't worry." My voice sounded to me like it was far away in a tunnel, as I explained. "You only have to put down five dollars, then it's two dollars a week after."

"Installment," Zoe said, blinking at the bags of candy in front of her.

We went up to the counter, and they chose rings. My headache was getting really bad, and I have to admit, I didn't love the way those rings looked on Morgan and Olivia. Not that there's anything wrong with or ugly about their hands. I don't know. I was just in a lousy mood. I tried to hide it by smiling a lot. I was relieved when Morgan and Olivia waved their ringed hands good-bye and headed back to Olivia's so Zoe and I could just sit on the curb and wait for my mother. We didn't talk, which was nice. Zoe's the kind of person who knows when you just need to not talk about it.

By three-ten I was in a panic.

fourteen

Mom showed up at quarter past three. I was a wreck but she was smiling so I figured I was safe. I climbed into the backseat with Zoe, who leaned forward to answer Mom's questions. I listened to the music of their voices mingling with the Tchaikovsky Mom had put on the cassette player.

Every time the phone rang the rest of the afternoon, I bolted to get it. One time I was in the bathroom — I didn't even flush, just ran into the hall yanking up my shorts. It was somebody wanting to know if we were interested in having our gutters cleaned.

"No, thank you," I said in a high voice, pretending to be my mother.

"This autumn's leaves can clog up the gutters and result in costly damage to your lovely house," the voice on the other end warned.

"My husband takes care of it himself," I said, hoping Dad does, and hung up.

"Your husband?" Zoe asked.

I shrugged and went back in to flush. We were supposedly doing some project in my room. Zoe was lying on my trundle bed, her arms behind her head, staring at the ceiling. I closed my door and sat in the corner, one leg against the door and one against the wall.

"Are you calling Tommy?" she asked me.

I stretched over my right leg. "Or I could just wait

until Monday to break up with him. You know, in person."

"Whatever you want," Zoe said. "You don't *have* to break up with him. I know, I mean, hay-stacking and everything. That was the point of all this. Right?"

"No," I said. "The point was to be with you. With everybody. To be normal and have fun. The point was fun. Remember?"

"Oh, yeah," she said. "Fun."

"If you think I'm going through all this just to get kissed, you're crazy."

"Yeah." She smiled. "He's not even supposed to be a good kisser."

I laughed, a little more than I meant to. It sort of came out a snort.

"Seriously," she said. "Isn't that why Morgan broke up with him last year?"

"She said Tommy practically broke her jaw off." Zoe and I both laughed hysterically. She snorted, too, which made me feel better. "Anyway, after what he did? I'm not, the last thing I want is to, we have to stick, I mean, you're my best friend."

Zoe played with the knot of her friendship ring. "Thanks."

"Are you mad?"

"About what?"

I stretched over my left leg, biting my knee. "About Morgan and Olivia?"

"What about them?" she asked without looking at me.

“About” — I sat up straight and looked at her, but she didn’t look back — “about, the rings.”

“No,” she said, but she didn’t sound positive.

“I just, I thought, I don’t know.” I dropped my head to the floor and rested my body there. “I’m sorry. I just want to please everybody, and I just, I mess everything up.”

Before she could answer the phone rang again. “I got it!” I yelled.

“Hello?” said the very familiar voice in my ear.

“Hi, Aunt Betsy,” I said, thinking, *Oh, no.* I brought the phone into my room and sat down next to Zoe on the trundle and mouthed, “It’s her.”

Meanwhile Aunt Betsy was saying, “Oh, hello, CJ. How are you?”

"Fine." I held up my hands to Zoe like what do I do? Zoe sat up and tucked her long hair behind her ears. "How are you?" I remembered to ask, a little late.

I wasn't really listening but I think she said she was fine and then asked to speak with Mom.

"Um," I said. Zoe was doing charades, but I wasn't sure what she meant I should say. Finally she pointed to my window. "She-she, my yard . . ."

"What?" Aunt Betsy asked.

I shook my head at Zoe, like *What?* Meanwhile, Zoe was rolling on the bed, laughing. "Out!" Zoe finally said.

"Out," I repeated, trying not to crack up myself.

"What did you say?" Aunt Betsy asked me, in her deep, raspy voice.

I cleared my throat. "She's out."

"Already?" Aunt Betsy asked.

"No," I blurted. Zoe's eyes opened wide. "Yes!" I corrected myself, then took a breath and said, "She's on her way out the door. So can, can she call you back tomorrow? She wants to know."

"Sure," Aunt Betsy answered. "Any time before five. We should be around all day."

"Great. 'Bye," I said, and hung up.

"Who was that?" Mom yelled from her bedroom.

"Um, Morgan!" I answered. Zoe and I stared at each other, frozen, waiting. Nothing happened. I lay down beside her, and we both stared at the ceiling. My head was pounding again.

Dad peeked in my door. "Girls?"

I sat up. "What?"

"We're going." Mom peeked in behind him. She was wearing her royal blue dress and her best clip in her French twist. She looked beautiful.

"Have fun," I said. "You guys look great."

"What do you have planned for tonight?" Mom asked us.

Zoe and I shrugged. "Nothing," I said.

"OK," said Mom. "Try to include Paul a little, though, please."

"No problem," said Zoe. "I'm the baby in my family, so I know."

"Be good," Dad said.

"Have fun," Mom said. They both blew kisses and then left.

Zoe and I lay back on the bed. "Sorry about this," I

said. "Just what you feel like doing, I bet — hanging around an eight-year-old all night."

"No," she said. "He's a great kid. And it's not like anybody's knocking down my telephone to ask me to do something exciting."

I almost said, *Except maybe Lou,* but I wasn't sure if we were quite ready to joke about that yet. "Well, thanks," I said instead. "I have a headache."

"Hey!" Zoe sat up. "Are we allowed to use the oven?"

I closed my eyes. "I guess. Why? They left us some fried chicken."

"I thought maybe we could bake something. That might be fun."

"Maybe," I said.

"Hey, Paul!" she yelled.

"What?" I heard him answer from his room.

"You want to bake cookies with us?"

"Yeah!" he yelled back. He was at my door looking like an excited puppy when I turned my head. "Really?"

"Sure." Zoe jumped off the bed and went to the door.

"Morgan always ignored me," Paul told her.

"I'm more fun than Morgan." Zoe looked back at me. "You coming?"

"My head really hurts," I mumbled and put my hand over my eyes. "I'll be down in a few. You start."

"OK!" Zoe pushed Paul toward the stairs. I was asleep before they got there.

fifteen

I was up really early this morning. Zoe was asleep in the trundle and my clock said five-seventeen. I just lay there for a few minutes not thinking until my life filled in and the panicky feeling came back. I crawled over Zoe who didn't notice at all, went to the bathroom, then tiptoed downstairs.

There was a huge platter full of cookies on the center island in the kitchen. I lifted the plastic wrap and chose one — it was light yellowish, and in the center was a small circle of jam. It was absolutely delicious. I sat on the steps with my feet propped against the banister and enjoyed it.

Mom sat down on the step above me. I hadn't even heard her coming.

"Ooo!" I said. We both jumped a little, then leaned against the wall with our feet up.

"You were asleep when I got home," Mom whispered. "Zoe told us she had to call her sister to come over with flour for the cookies."

"Really?"

"Embarrassing. What kind of house has no flour?"

I didn't answer her.

Mom ran her fingers through her wet hair and said, "Zoe is really sweet. Paul was pretending to be asleep when we got home, but he was smiling so much he couldn't fool us at all. She really won him over."

I finished the cookie.

"You want to do your stretches in the living room?"

Mom offered. "I'm going to bring Daddy some coffee, and then I'll come sit with you."

"OK," I said.

When she got down, I was on my back with my feet over my head. "What if I never make principal dancer?" I asked her when she was settled on the couch. It was my new plan, my way to tell her I was quitting.

"As long as you give it your all, I'm satisfied." It's not what she was supposed to say.

I pushed the stretch harder as the *Swan Lake* music she chose came on. My next planned sentence was, "I wouldn't be satisfied either, and since I don't think I'm going to make principal dancer . . ." so I was a little lost.

"But I think you really might, CJ," she said, perching

on the edge of the couch. "When I see you dance, it's like, well, it's like every dream of mine has come true. You've looked especially beautiful this week, so graceful, such a natural. You've really got something special."

So I didn't tell her. Again.

By ten o'clock, everybody was up and rushing around. Dad had left for his golf game, and Mom was running late as usual for showing a house. "How many times have I shown this house?" she asked Paul.

"I don't know." Paul was sitting next to Zoe on the couch, watching cartoons.

"Where are my keys?" she asked me.

I shrugged.

"Oh, and I have to call Aunt Betsy! Where's the phone?"

Zoe and I looked at each other. Nobody answered Mom.

"How many times . . ." Mom started, dashing into then out of the kitchen. "We have to make a family rule that the phone gets put back on the charger thing when you're done with it."

I spotted the phone on top of the microwave. Mom was moving in that direction, getting warmer, warmer . . . "I think I left it upstairs," I yelled, and jumped up from the chair to dash up the stairs, yelling, "Sorry!"

"Don't run," Mom said automatically. I slowed down and walked up the steps.

I heard Mom grab her keys, I don't know where from. "CJ! I only have a minute!"

I was standing at the top of the stairs not knowing what to do. If I did nothing, I was afraid she'd look around again, find the phone, and Aunt Betsy would tell. I had to think fast. Only one thing occurred to me as a possible stalling tactic — I had to throw myself down the steps.

Paul and I used to do it all the time, just roll down the steps — pretending we were stuntmen. I was smaller then, though, and I hadn't spent so much time learning to be careful not to hurt myself. The past few years I've learned to hold onto banisters, avoid loose steps, not jump across puddles. I take the long way around. I never run; you could twist an ankle and be out for weeks. If you're going to dance, you have to protect your body.

I stood up at the top of the stairs and imagined heaving myself down, headfirst. I tried to, then grabbed the banister before I fell. *If I twist an ankle,* I told myself, *I'll get out of dance!* Of course, no way she'll let me go apple picking or play soccer if I'm hobbling around on crutches anyway. Oh, what to do? I squeezed my eyes shut and tried to think fast. *Don't think,* I told myself, *just fall.* I counted to three and tried again, but my body wouldn't let me.

"CJ! Did you find it?"

I was left with only the most desperate tactic in the world — the be stupid stall. "Find what?"

"The phone! Oh! Here it is!"

I ran down the stairs. "Don't run," Mom mumbled, setting the phone on the charger. "We don't need you getting hurt, with *Nutcracker* auditions coming up."

"Sorry."

Mom pulled her glasses out of her pocketbook, stuck them on top of her head, and gave a kiss to Paul, who pulled away, looking at Zoe.

I heard myself ask, "You're not calling Aunt Betsy?"

"I'm late. If she calls, tell her I just had to run out for a while and I'll try to get her before dinner, OK?"

"OK."

She kissed my forehead and then Zoe's. Zoe looked a little surprised. She said, "Thanks!"

Mom backed through the door, thanking Zoe for the cookies and for taking such good care of Paul. Zoe waved her hand like it was nothing, and the three of us watched out the window as Mom sprinted to her car.

Zoe turned to me and said, "Close call."

"What?" Paul asked.

Zoe and I looked at each other and started to laugh. "Hey, Paul?" Zoe asked. "Want to have a catch?"

"Yeah," he said.

I ate another cookie and prayed for the people my mom was with to have a lot, lot of questions.

sixteen

I could tell Dad had stopped paying attention. He was still alternating saying uh-huh and shaking his head when Mom paused, but like a half-second too late. Paul and I looked at each other. We knew Dad was in for it.

"So the whole deal is going to fall through," Mom said, spearing a piece of chicken savagely with her fork.

Dad shook his head. He was staring past her, toward the sprinkler over in his vegetable garden. I was a little more relaxed than I'd been so far in the weekend because my family has a Family Night rule for Sunday nights — no phone calls after five. I was safe for the night.

"I mean," Mom continued with her mouth full. "I can't believe I spent the entire day there. I think a lien on the house is something you ought to mention to the real estate agent at some point, don't you think?"

This time Dad forgot to say uh-huh, so Mom looked at me and Paul. We both nodded seriously, as if we had any clue what she was saying. But we both know when Mom starts talking with her mouth full, you just shut up and agree.

"Unbelievable! So now after all this work, I mean, how many people did I march through that house? How many times can I possibly point out the fabulous possibilities of that cruddy waterlogged basement?"

"Mmm," Dad said, helping himself to more peas.

Mom opened her mouth and touched her side upper teeth with her tongue, staring at Dad.

"Uh-oh," I whispered to Paul. He smiled a little at me. He loves when I pay attention to him, which I should, more. Zoe had, and he's practically ready to hang posters of her in his room.

"So then I bought a pig," Mom said. "And painted the kitchen purple. Don't you agree?"

"Definitely," Dad said, nodding and turning to look at her. When he saw the look on her face, he knew he was caught. "What?" he asked innocently.

Mom slammed down her silverware, grabbed the bowl of peas, and marched off into the house.

"Did she say something about a pig?" Dad asked me and Paul.

We nodded.

"Oh, no." Dad slapped himself on the forehead. "I just, the vegetables, the sprinklers were . . ." His mustache bounced up and down as he talked, so only his bottom teeth showed.

"Mmm-hmm," I said.

"Don't you start, too."

Mom stomped back out to the deck and grabbed our plates. Paul, the slowest eater in America, hadn't finished his rice or chicken, but he didn't say anything. He just grabbed his drumstick as his plate was moving away from him and scrunched down in his chair to nibble on it.

"As if I . . . forget it," Mom grumbled and stormed back inside.

"Dad?" I asked, picking up his plate gently. "It's just one dance class, and this is the only trip . . ."

"Oh, no," Dad said, taking his plate away from me. "I'm already in enough trouble. You talk to your mother."

Dad followed Mom in and closed the sliding door. I looked glumly at Paul, about to explain to him about soccer and dance and the apple-picking trip, because, well, Zoe gets help with her problems from her four older sisters. Even though he's only eight, I was thinking maybe he could be a friend to me. "I really want to go on this trip," I told him. "I hate ballet."

"So do I."

"You do?"

"Nobody pays any attention to me. Except Zoe. I wish you'd quit."

"I'm trying," I whispered. "Don't say anything."

"I don't even know what's going on," he said. "Want to have a catch?"

"No," I said, picking up the glasses. It's stupid to think a younger brother could understand.

I closed the sliding door with my foot while Paul complained, "Won't anybody have a catch with me? I've been waiting all day! I wish Zoe were my sister."

"Everything is not about you, Paul," I yelled back. He didn't answer, so then I felt bad. He had been waiting all day. "I'll play with you later, OK?"

By the time I got to the kitchen door, Mom was slamming plates into the sink. "Wait around all day for you," she was saying, narrowing her eyes at my father. I pressed myself against the living room wall so she wouldn't see me. "And what do you do, golf? All day? How important is that? Paul's been holding that football since ten this morning. So we can't go apple picking, even though it's so important to her, so I tell them I can fill in for work, and then when I try to tell you the biggest deal this month is falling apart, you, what were you staring at anyway?"

"The sprinkler," Dad muttered.

"The sprinkler?" Mom was even more furious. "The sprinkler?"

"It looked stuck," Dad said.

"The sprinkler. Unbelievable. At least have the intelligence to lie!"

"You want me to lie?" Dad asked. I waited to hear the answer.

"Some huge thing at work?" Mom suggested. "Or how about, you were feeling guilty about ruining your whole family's weekend? The sprinkler?"

"I didn't want to overwater," Dad said. I peeked around the corner. He was standing behind Mom, putting his arms around her waist while she squeezed soap into the sink. She elbowed him. "Ow!" he said, and she cracked a little smile.

When he pushed her out of the way to take over washing the dishes, I knew it was safe to go in. I placed the glasses carefully on the counter next to Mom, who was sitting up there like we're not allowed to.

"Mom?"

She looked at me like, *Now what?* I started thinking, *Well, maybe just forget it.* My throat was a little scratchy anyway, maybe I should just stay home sick tomorrow, miss the trip, miss dance class, miss everything in my whole life. But no — you have to be practically dying in my family. She sent Paul to school with chicken pox as soon as they crusted last year. Besides, what about soccer? At some point, she was going to have to be told all this stuff, and the perfect opportunity kept not coming.

"What, CJ?"

Paul wandered in from outside and left the sliding door open.

"I was thinking about the apple-picking trip," I said slowly.

Mom looked up at the corner of the ceiling like that was the only spot in the world that understood what she goes through. "You made a commitment, CJ!"

I felt my jaw jut out over my front teeth. "But," I whispered. "I just, I thought, it's the only time . . ."

"CJ, I'm not arguing with you," she said, jumping down off the counter and stalking through the kitchen and living room. "Besides, you already made the arrangements for in-school study."

I didn't say anything.

"Didn't you?"

"Yes, yes, yes!" I yelled. "Don't you even trust me?"

"Of course I do."

"You don't act it," I mumbled, down to the kitchen floor.

Mom slapped her legs. "CJ, don't make me feel like I'm forcing you into this."

"Sorry."

She slammed the sliding glass door shut and stepped back over Paul, who was sprawled across the living room floor, watching a very loud football game. "You know how we feel about breaking commitments, CJ," Mom said as she came toward me. "If you'd grown up on a farm, you'd know there's no such thing as you don't feel like it. The cows need to be milked every day, no matter what." She looked me right in the eyes, and I realized she's not so much taller than I am anymore.

"I know," I said, pushing my arch by pressing the top of my foot against the wood of the kitchen floor. "But, Dad?"

Dad lifted his wet hands out of the sink, like he was surrendering. "Uh-uh," he said. "I was listening. I was paying attention. I agreed with Mom. The cows need to be milked every day, and so do you."

I stared down at my bare feet, covered in calluses, my long, narrow feet pointing away from each other, in perfect second position without my even thinking about it. My turn-out has definitely been improving, maybe as good as Morgan's now, if not better. Leaving the kitchen, I glanced up at the cow-shaped kitchen clock. Thirteen hours.

seventeen

She told me how proud she is of me as she kissed me good night and said, “It’s really hard sometimes, huh?”

I nodded and rolled over, away from my mother, to face the wall. She caressed my hair back from my forehead like I love. How can she be so understanding and still not understand me? *Rain*, I prayed. *If it rains tomorrow, they’ll have to cancel the trip, and I won’t have to deal with this until the next day, for soccer practice.*

She leaned over to kiss my forehead, then pulled up my quilt and walked across my room. I flipped to watch her. My old stuffed animals were all lined up on the top shelf in a neat row the way she likes, except History. He had slumped over onto Curious George. She picked up History and fluffed him, then sat him up in a cute pose with his front paws between his back ones.

"I love you," she said, flipping off my light. She closed my door just the right amount.

I stared at History and prayed for rain. A few minutes went by. I whispered "I love you" because I got scared maybe it would be bad luck not to; I say it every night. I could hear Mom's and Dad's voices downstairs but not their words, and when they laughed, I felt like they were laughing at me. It's not funny! I wanted to yell. I got angrier and angrier. Minutes ticked by on my clock. I looked up at History. He was still sitting there in his cute pose with his front paws between his back ones. I used to carry him around all the time. Mom named him Doggie, but I said no, his name is History.

Well, that's the story my parents tell, anyway. They thought that was so cute, they even called my grandma Nelly, which Mom never does, to tell her. I remember vaguely being on the phone telling her, "My new dog's name is History," or maybe I only remember the story. My parents like to tell the same story over and over again, like how my mom grew up on a dairy farm, doing thick-booted chores in poop and milk drippings before dawn, fantasizing, while she mucked, of escaping to dance like a swan in the spotlight at Lincoln Center and then three days after her seventeenth birthday, instead of buying a dozen eggs and a jar of apple butter, she kept walking and used her grocery money plus what she'd hoarded over the years for a bus ticket. It's sort of like praying — you just say the words again and again and it's this thing you do. *God bless Mommy and Daddy and Paul and me,* so if you add *Please make it rain,* the "please make it rain" part is the only part that feels like asking for something — the rest is just what you say as you close your eyes.

I don't even know what's true and what's just the words. I kind of doubt a two-and-a-half-year-old would come up with the name History for her stuffed animal, especially me, who had such trouble talking anyway. In fact, they said I hardly talked at all before I was three — the quietest, sweetest little girl ever, goes that story. So no way did I come up with that name myself.

I sat up and punched my pillow, totally furious that they've deceived me all these years. How can I learn to be honest in a family like this? Mom even told Dad tonight that he should lie. What are they trying to teach us?

I looked up at History in his cute pose. It felt like he's not even mine, like he's a spy in my room, and I don't even know what I would really want to call him. I stomped over to my shelves even though I wasn't supposed to be out of my bed and shoved him over. He slumped onto Curious George again.

I got back in bed and squeezed my eyes shut.

eighteen

No rain.

When Mom woke me up to do my stretching, it took me about a second before I looked out my window. "Beautiful day," Mom said. I flopped back down, thinking a word I am not allowed to say.

While I stretched, I tried to figure out what to do. If I admit to having forged the permission slip, she'll kill me. If I don't admit it and just go on the trip, so I'm picking apples when she shows up at two-forty, she'll kill me. She never lets me fake and stay home sick; I'd have to come up with a broken bone or something. For a minute, I tried to decide what bone to break and how, but Mom popped her head in and said breakfast was ready, so she'd seen me whole already and wouldn't be convinced. What then? I could just not go on the trip, but I'd already turned in the permission slip, so there's no way the teachers or Mrs. Johnson, the principal, would let me not go. Mom would find out what I did and kill me.

I ended my stretching with the foot bands. I hadn't come up with a solution. Paul knocked on my door. "Do you have dance class today?"

"I always have dance on Monday!" I yelled at him.

"Fine!" He yelled back. "Fine! So it's not my fault if I don't have my project done, because Mom is always with you!"

He slammed my door. "What project?" I heard Mom ask.

"It's due tomorrow," Paul said. "I have to go to the fire station and talk to three firefighters."

I pulled on a white T-shirt and my overalls, while I listened. Dad was asking Paul, "When did this assignment get assigned? This morning?"

"Forget it," mumbled Paul. I tugged some fluffy yellow socks on and wiggled my Keds on top. I couldn't wait to get out there and eavesdrop, so I quickly opened my door and went to the bathroom to put up my own hair. Mom and Dad had followed Paul into his room and were arguing about who would be able to take Paul to the fire station. Dad had a big meeting at three and he couldn't say how long it would be, and of course Mom was planning to take me to dance class. I kept my mouth shut. What could I do? Offer to not go so she could take Paul? But then she would realize about the permission slip and have a fit, unless I could think of some way to tell her somebody else's mother could pick me up or something. But she would say no because of dance. The whole thing was too complicated, so I just had to stop thinking and smooth my frizzy hair into a tight bun, tuck in all the loose ends.

I gobbled down my bowl of cereal and waited out by the car while Mom was tugging Paul's shirt over his head. He's eight years old! I wanted to scream. Let him dress himself, no wonder he doesn't take responsibility for his own assignments. But of course I didn't say anything, just leaned against the car looking up at the crystal-clear sky thinking, *What a perfect day for apple picking*, and, *maybe the bus will crash and I'll die and not have to face the consequences.*

"Your dance bag," Mom said.

"What?"

A strand of her hair was hanging down over her eyes, and her pocketbook fell off her shoulder onto her elbow, which jolted her coffee cup so some spilled on her white Ked.

"CJ, please," she said, stamping her foot, tucking back her hair, opening the car door, and throwing her pocketbook in. "Don't go spacey on me today. Go get your dance bag so it will be in the car when I pick you up this afternoon."

I stood there for a second thinking, *Oh, my God. This can't be happening. There has to be a way out. What am I going to do?*

"Earth to CJ," Paul said.

"Shut up," I said, hating him for his pretty face and lack of responsibilities. I mean, honestly, if I had left the sliding door open last night, my mother would've killed me. She never expects anything of Paul. He doesn't even have to say excuse me when he gets up from the table. He doesn't have to dance for her.

"CJ," Mom said. "Please."

I looked at her. Her dark green eyes rested on mine, and for a second I felt like she was reading my mind, like she knew what my plan was. Like she was saying, *Please, admit to me what you were thinking of doing because I know anyway and it's fine — go, have a good time, I want you to.*

"Please what?" I asked.

She rolled her head back and looked at the sky. "Aaah! Your dance bag! Come on, CJ. I have an appointment in twenty minutes!"

So she didn't know.

Too complicated to think of a solution, I told myself as I pulled open the back door. *In too deep to get out, no use worrying now.* I picked up my dance bag. *Maybe it will all work itself out later.*

Halfway down the stairs I remembered my new pink leg warmers were drying over the shower rod. I walked back up the steps, pushed open the bathroom door, put my dance bag on the floor, and pulled the leg warmers down. They were dry and even softer than before. I folded them carefully, then unzipped my dance bag and placed them inside, on top of my toe shoes. I zipped the bag closed, wondering when I would open it next, and walked downstairs and out again to the car.

nineteen

I opened the car door before Mom had even stopped. We were both looking at the apple-picking bus, the huge gray bus waiting in the circle with its motor running. I didn't want to get into a discussion. It was too late.

"So it's all arranged?" Mom asked. "The independent —"

"Yes." I slammed the door shut and waved without looking at her. Morgan was already waiting beside the bus. She waved at me with her friendship-ringed hand. I waved back and said, "Just have to go to my locker," pointing at my bag. She nodded.

I walked slowly down the hall to my locker and dialed my combination carefully. It was still neat; I like to try to keep my locker neat as long as possible. I lined up my books carefully inside, taking them one by one out of my bag, and positioned my homework folder between my math text and my Spanish. I almost set my lunch on the shelf, where I always put it, then remembered I should take it with me, because, obviously, we wouldn't be here for lunch. I peeked inside to see what lunch I'd gotten and saw there was a note from Mom. It said, *Love you.* I crumpled it and dropped it in my locker, which I slammed shut.

I carefully dialed my locker combination again, opened it, and picked up the note. I smoothed it, folded it in quarters, and stuck it in my overalls pocket. Then

I slammed my locker shut again and sprinted back outside.

By the time I got there, most of the other kids had arrived. Morgan, Olivia, and Zoe were standing together, so I went right over to them.

"Did you do it?" Morgan asked.

How did she find out? "What?" I asked.

"Break up with Tommy?"

I'd forgotten all about him. "Oh, um."

"You didn't?" She looked at Olivia and Zoe, shocked and disappointed.

"I just, I didn't get the chance," I explained.

Morgan rested her hands on her hips and asked, "But you don't like him anymore, do you?"

"Oh, no. No way."

I heard sneakers crunching on the pebbles behind me and spun around to see Tommy's back, scooting away. I covered my mouth. "Do you think he heard?"

"Do you care?" Morgan asked.

"Well," offered Zoe. "Still, you wouldn't want to . . ."

"What?" Morgan asked, turning to Zoe. "You're the one he made a fool of. You of all people shouldn't stick up for him."

Zoe shrugged. "Let's get on the bus and compare junk food."

Relieved, I followed her on. We chose seats near the back, across from each other — me and Zoe in one seat, Morgan and Olivia in the other, and dug through our bags. With our heads down near our knees, Zoe whispered to me, "Did you talk to your mother?"

"No," I admitted.

"What's going to happen?"

I shook my head. "I don't know."

"Are we not talking about it?"

"Right," I said.

She gave me some Cheez Doodles.

twenty

What a great day. The actual apple picking felt almost beside the point. We each filled up a bag pretty quickly, and since the rule is you can eat as many as you want, everybody except poor sore Olivia did a lot of eating, too. I'm not sure who started it — Morgan, I think — but it quickly became a "thing" to take a bite of an apple, spit it out, and say, "Sour." We thought we were a real riot, doing that. Even the boys did it. The whole seventh grade. Mrs. Shepard, the English/social studies teacher who is very sour herself, told us we were all disgusting. We loved it. We think Ms.

Cress was laughing, no matter how serious she tried to look to impress Mrs. Shepard. Zoe said at least we'd all achieved unity in being disgusting.

A skinny, enthusiastic guy with a huge Adam's apple and a red name tag announcing MY NAME IS LARRY! wrote our names on our bags. We each said, "Thanks, Larry!" as we left the bags beside him in the barn and went to drink apple cider (sour!) and listen to some hokey music.

"Come on," Larry! yelled, skipping out of the barn. "Everybody square dance!"

We were all hanging back, rolling our eyes, like, *Do they honestly expect us to square dance? Please.* But then Larry! grabbed Zoe who grabbed Morgan on her way out and they got really into it so everybody else joined in, too. It wasn't like ballet at all. Nobody cared about the beauty of your line and how long your neck looked or how high your legs got. Nobody really looked at anybody. We were all just laughing. I tripped over Lou's foot one time, and it wasn't even weird. I said, "Sorry," and he said, "You clod," and I said, "Look who's talking," and he looked at himself and pretended to be surprised. Then we switched partners and I had Tommy, which I admit was a little awkward. I tried to think of something to say, but as usual I couldn't, so I just do-si-doed him and went on with my day.

After the square dancing Larry! yelled, "Time to line up for the three-legged race!" He and two perky women with bandanna headbands started cheering, totally psyched. When we have three-legged races in gym, nobody in our grade wants to do it. My grade is just like that — when grown-ups get gung-ho, we get turned off. The grade ahead of us gets totally into everything — like

Olivia's gorgeous thirteen-year-old brother, Dex, is always organizing cleanup drives and charity auctions. My grade, when they announce three-legged races in gym, we all develop stomachaches, and if they force us, we just walk as slow as we can.

Especially me. A three-legged race is the perfect way to twist your ankle. I have never in my life strapped my leg to another person's to try running. It's insane.

But there we were, grabbing at the ties. I grabbed. Zoe and I were laughing as we pulled the ties tighter on our ankles and calves. I was psyched, I really was.

Tommy and Jonas ran by us strapped together, yelling, "Don't even bother!"

"You'd better watch out!" Zoe yelled back. She shrugged at me. "Now we have to win."

"It's not even fair," I pointed out as I wrapped my arm around her waist. "They're twins. They're exactly the same size."

We tried moving but fell immediately. My first thought was, *Did I twist anything?* But my next was, *Who cares?* It felt like fresh air was pumped into my body, just to be able to think, who cares? I jumped up and dragged Zoe out of the dirt.

"Your bun," Zoe said.

I lifted my hand and felt my frizzy hair coming loose. I tried to smooth it down, shove the stray pieces in, and clip them with the silver clips on the side. "Is it better?" I asked Zoe.

"Well . . ." she said. "Um . . ."

"Forget it," I said. I took out the clips and dropped

them on the ground, pulled off my new flowered scrunchie and looped it around my wrist. Tommy and Jonas were whizzing past us again. I yelled, "We're leaving you in our dust!"

"Yeah!" Zoe said, pointing after them. That tipped us out of balance, and we toppled over again.

"Is my hair blocking your vision?" I asked her.

"It cushioned my fall," she said.

Morgan and Olivia limped over, tied to each other. Olivia put a hand out to us, which Zoe grabbed. I had a dirt smudge on my sleeve and one on the knee of my overalls. I liked how that looked, so I didn't bother wiping it clean, and anyway my Keds were filthy; I must've stepped in something. My hair felt huge. I pushed it down, but it's very boingy, so it doesn't go down easily.

"You guys know how to do this?" Morgan asked.

"Sure," Zoe said. "We're a machine."

"Yeah," said Olivia. "You look like you're getting the hang of it."

"You, too," I said. Then we all cracked up.

Our buddy Larry! blew his whistle. We all yelled, "Larry!" as we hobbled over to the starting line. Somehow we managed to get there still on our feet. Morgan and Olivia were next to me; Tommy and Jonas were on the other side of Zoe.

"On your marks," Larry! said.

"You die," I heard Tommy growl to Zoe.

"You wish," Zoe said back.

"Get set!"

"Wait — my left or your left?" Morgan asked Olivia.

"Go!"

The whistle blew and we were off. We were running,

galloping, Zoe and I, in a rhythm together, keeping up, passing Tommy and Jonas, all the way to the line at the other side. "We win!" I yelled, throwing my arms into the air. I never felt so purely happy.

Until Zoe fell on top of me.

"Turn!" she yelled on our way down. "We have to go back!"

"Back?" I twisted, following her to the ground, and as we fell I noticed that the other pairs were turning around to go back to the starting line. I must have missed that part of the rules.

Tommy and Jonas made the turn smoothly, but Olivia and Morgan were falling, too, or maybe they would've been OK if I hadn't knocked into them. By the time the dust started settling on top of our human pile, Larry! had come over to disentangle us.

He scooped up Morgan first. She said, "Larry!"

His Adam's apple bounced around as he lifted Olivia, then me. Somehow my free leg had gotten twisted around Zoe's head, so that her face was in the dirt. When I saw that, I stopped laughing.

"Are you OK?" I asked her.

She lifted her head. There was dirt from the tip of her nose down to the bottom of her chin. She looked awful. I felt my hand go up to my chest. "Oh, Zoe," I said.

She spit, smiled, and said, "Sour."

twenty-one

We sat on top of a haystack, drinking lemonades. The four of us had decided we didn't want any souvenirs, so while everyone else was scrambling around the gift shop in the last few minutes before getting back on the bus, we sat up high on the otherwise unused haystacks, sipping our lemonades and just feeling happy.

Same seats on the ride back, so I stared out the window with Zoe beside me. I crossed my legs. It felt weird but sort of ladylike. I watched the trees and telephone poles go by and didn't think about anything, my forehead pressed against the cold window. At one point Zoe offered me an apple. I said, "Oof." She smiled and I smiled.

The bus groaned as it made the turn onto the driveway of school. We were tired and dirty and full, but all, I think, pretty happy. Nobody had hay-stacked, but if the whole point is doing something to unite the seventh grade at the beginning of the year, well, it had.

Mrs. Johnson was waiting in the circle, her normally friendly face wrinkled and harsh. And, worse, right behind her were Mom and Dad, with their hands on their hips. I closed my eyes.

Kids were standing before the bus made its *tst* sound and stopped completely. Bags of apples were dragged out from under seats, and the aisle was filled, though some kids were looking out the windows to see if their parents were here yet or late. I sat, eyes closed. *One more minute,* I wished for.

Mrs. Johnson pushed against the tide of tired seventh graders, up onto the bus. "CJ?"

I lifted my head and met her eyes.

"You march your pretty little self down the aisle. This instant," Mrs. Johnson said. Then she turned to the teachers. "I tried to call you on the cell phone. You never answered."

Ms. Cress said, "I never heard . . ." She dug it out of her bag and looked at it, saying, "Oops."

"Is something wrong?" I heard Mrs. Shepard whisper.

I was starting to pull my bag of apples out from under my seat, but Zoe whispered, "I'll get 'em for you." She stood beside our seats to let me out, tucking her hair behind her ears. I could tell she wanted to say something helpful. I took a deep breath and she took one, too. When I looked over at Olivia and Morgan, they were staring back, worried about me. That felt good, at least. I lowered my head and squeezed down the aisle toward Mrs. Johnson, thinking as my arms brushed other kids' arms, *Well, this is it.* As I walked, I pulled my hair back into a ponytail in my scrunchie, because I didn't need my parents seeing me looking quite so wild. I stepped over Lou's bag of apples at the front of the bus and could smell Mrs. Johnson's perfume, clean as white sheets.

She grabbed me by the elbow and growled, "I'm appalled at your behavior." She pulled me down the bus steps. "You have some explaining to do to your parents. And I'll see you at eight o'clock tomorrow morning in my office." She yanked me across the black concrete up onto the sidewalk, where my parents were waiting. My mother's face was red, my father's was white.

Mom grabbed me out of Mrs. Johnson's grip, hugged me hard, then stared at my face. The most frightening part was, I couldn't tell what in the world she was thinking. Usually I can spot any thought flickering for a second across my mother's face; I've spent my whole life looking into it like my own personal crystal ball. But it was cloudy as she stared into my eyes, and that even more than the yelling I was braced for made me feel like I might fall down.

Other kids were thumping out of the bus, jumping down off the bus's step, and glancing over at me. I could feel them doing it and could hear them whispering: "What happened?" "What did she do?" Everybody was going to know. Out of the corner of my vision, I saw Ms.

Cress and Mrs. Shepard looking up at Mrs. Johnson, who was telling them, "I'll fill you in later. Right now let's send everybody home happy." The sun had just set, so the sky was turning pink and orange behind the line of jeeps and minivans lined up waiting to take home kids and apples. Someone beeped. I looked to see who it was.

Mom cupped my chin and yanked it back toward her. "Don't you turn away from me." Her voice was quiet and fierce.

"Sorry," I whispered.

"What were you thinking?" Dad asked.

I didn't answer.

He asked again. "What were you thinking? What?"

Nothing, I thought. I had decided not to think. But there was no way to explain that, so I just looked at my shoes, my muddy grayish-brown Keds.

"I don't even know where to start, CJ," Mom whispered. "Tell me where we should start. With what I was thinking, waiting here for you at two-forty, when you never came out? At three, when I finally went in to school looking for you and Mrs. Johnson informed me that you had never arranged independent study, that you had gone apple picking? That I had signed a permission slip? I! Signed it. Did I sign that permission slip, CJ? Did I?"

"No," I admitted.

"Who signed it? Who signed my name?"

"I did," I said.

Dad grabbed me by both arms and shook me. "Do you know that it's a crime to forge another person's signature? You could go to jail. Look at me."

I tried to lift my eyes to meet his. I got as far as his belt with the silver square buckle Paul and I had bought him for his birthday.

"Look at me!" he screamed.

I looked up into his furious face. I could tell he hated me, and I didn't blame him. "We've been sitting here worried to death about you," he yelled, shaking me. "Your mother called me, frantic. I had to run out of my meeting and stand here waiting and praying that my lying, cheating, conniving daughter really did go to pick apples and wasn't lying dead in a ditch somewhere."

"I'm sorry."

"'I'm sorry' isn't going to begin to solve this." He turned to Mom. "I'm going in to call the baby-sitter. Paul was near hysteria, last time we called."

Mom nodded, and we watched Dad stalk toward the school. He threw open the door so hard I thought it might fly off the hinges, and my dad is not a muscle man at all. He's very gentle, normally. And careful. He's an architect. He always puts pen caps back on. I twitched when the door slammed shut behind him.

Mom stared at me again but didn't say anything. I could tell she had lost all respect for me. She would be right never to trust me again, or like me, or love me. I had lied, Dad was right. I lied, and I went behind their backs, and I made them worry, just being selfish. Just because I felt like going with my friends. What a terrible person I am.

Headlights passed over me and Mom as cars pulled away. "'Bye!" kids shouted out windows to one other, and maybe to me. One car pulled into the circle and stopped beside us. When I heard the electric window buzzing down, I turned just my eyes, I couldn't help it, and saw it was Olivia and her mother. Aunt Betsy leaned across tiny Olivia, who was buckled into the front seat beside her. "Corey," she called to Mom. "Everything OK?"

Mom nodded. "Thanks."

"OK," said Aunt Betsy, closing the window and slowly pulling away.

Mom was staring at the sky when I dared look at her again. I wondered if she was trying not to cry, if she learned that looking-up trick from me or if I had learned it from her. Another car tooted pleasantly. "The entire town," she mumbled. "Every single . . ." She took a breath and shook her head before she looked down into my eyes again. "Go wait in the car, please, CJ. I don't want to look at you right now."

I tried to think of anything in the world to do or say to

make it better, but there was nothing. She had never before in my life not wanted to look at me. I turned to walk toward the car and noticed my head was hanging down, my shoulders were rounded, my belly was poufed out. I

knew that I was ugly, knew that Mom and everybody could see how ugly I really was. It felt worse than I had even last year when I auditioned for the part of Clara in *The Nutcracker* and stood there with the other finalists with Mom watching and a number on my chest, when Yuri said, "Thank you, number seventeen. Good-bye." And Mom had cried, a little. She denied it, but I saw a tear. *Not good enough,* I told myself then, and every time I saw Fiona in her Clara costume. Ugly, awkward, clumsy. *Practice more,* Mom had suggested to me cheerily. *Stretch harder, I'll wake you every day at dawn, and next year we'll show 'em at* The Nutcracker *auditions. Eat less,* I told myself, *concentrate better — or quit. Who needs this anyway? I don't want to be Clara anyway, I'd rather be normal, hang out at the pizza place with my friends, so I don't care.*

But this time, opening the car door and slumping into the backseat, there were no words to make me feel better. Eating less or stretching more wouldn't solve anything. I tried deciding, so what? I don't want Mom and Dad to love me anyway. But it's not true. I slammed the car door shut to hide my ugly self.

twenty-two

When we got home, Paul was waiting on the porch. I got out of the silent car and trudged up to the porch, ready for Paul to tell me how dead I was. Instead he hugged me and whispered, "Don't run away."

"What?" I asked, but Mom and Dad had caught up and Dad said, "Straight upstairs."

In my room, I pulled History down from my shelf, but then I decided, *No, I don't deserve the comfort.* I slumped into the little space between my dresser and the wall, not thinking, just feeling really, really pathetic, and listening to my family eating dinner quietly below me.

I heard the sink go on, which meant they were done, and then I heard Mom's footsteps coming up the stairs. I sunk down lower, happy she was coming but at the same time, not.

She opened my door slowly, and I could tell she was looking around for me. My feet were sticking out, so I stretched them a little, and she came over. She placed a plate of turkey and carrots and French fries on my floor between us.

"Hungry?" she asked. Even sitting cross-legged on the floor my mother looks graceful and elegant, with her pearl earrings and perfect posture.

"No," I whispered. "Thank you." I tried to sit up

straight. I had pulled the pretty flowered scrunchie off my hair and left it up on my dresser, so my hair filled most of the space around me. I didn't care how ugly I looked anymore.

"CJ," Mom said. "We have to talk."

"I know." I closed my eyes and leaned back against the wall for a second, practicing the words I'd been preparing. "I know I was bad," I started.

"No," Mom said quietly. "You're not a little child anymore, CJ. You weren't just bad, it's not that simple."

I started to cry. "I know."

"I feel just terrible, CJ, and I haven't even begun to sort this out, but I think the first thing, the worst thing to me is, it's clear to me that we haven't been communicating, and that's at least partly my fault."

"Your fault?"

"Why didn't you tell me you wanted so desperately to go on this trip?"

"I tried, Mom," I told her.

"I guess I wasn't really hearing you."

I covered my face with my hands. "Don't," I said.

"Mrs. Johnson has your name down on a list to play soccer. Were you planning to discuss that with me?"

I shrugged, my face still hidden. I wished she would just punish me, or spank me, or tell me I'm grounded until I'm forty-two. I sunk down lower into my body.

"Is that — is that instead of ballet?"

I shrugged again.

"You have to talk to me, CJ," she said, pulling my hands down. It was dark now in my room, only the light from the lamppost outside by the sidewalk streaming in, throwing Mom's shadow long and thin across my floor. "What do you want, CJ? I'm asking you and I want to listen. Do you want to dance?"

I didn't answer. I couldn't. I didn't know what the answer should be. I only knew she wanted me to dance and my friends didn't want me to.

"What do you want?" she asked again. "Is it hard to talk? I love you, I mean to be here for you, it should be OK to tell me anything. I'm sorry. I guess I haven't been a very good mother to you lately."

"No!" I hadn't meant to yell and usually my voice is pretty quiet, so it startled us both. "No," I said again. "You're a great mother, but don't do that to me, don't turn everything around, I can't keep up."

"What do you mean?" she asked, tilting her head to the side and waiting, now, listening.

"I mean, I-I-I can't, the rest of you, you can all, you're so much more Word than I am."

She nodded a little and waited.

"I can't, the words just, for me, I-I get so turned around when I talk to you I don't remember what I was trying to say, and then I just, I mean, all I know is I want to make you happy, but . . ."

"But you have to do what's right for yourself, too," she filled in.

I nodded.

"And what's right for you?"

I just shrugged.

"Well, you must have something in mind."

"Wait," I begged. "Just . . ."

She sucked her lips into her mouth and waited.

"I know I was bad, or, not bad, but I was, what Daddy said — lying, cheating, horrible . . ."

Mom shook her head. "He didn't say horrible. He was scared. And surprised and disappointed."

"I know." I rested my face in my hands.

"I'm sorry," she whispered. "Go ahead. So? What is right for you? Playing soccer? Do you even like soccer?"

"No!" I pulled my knees up to my chest and hid my face between them. "But it's not soccer, or picking apples, it's just, Mom? I'm not like you."

She didn't say anything for a minute, and neither did I. That had just popped out, but there it hung, between us. Finally she asked, "In what way?"

I couldn't look up at her but now that it was there, I had to finish. I stared at the dark floor between my knees and told her, "I'm not . . . You always wanted to be special, and you are, you are a superstar, with style and special, spotlights. Everywhere you go, it's like there's a . . . Whether you danced at Lincoln Center or not, it's just, you stand out from the crowd, everybody looks at you when you walk in a room. But I don't, do that, or, want that. I want to be *in* the crowd. I just want to be regular. Don't say no you don't."

"OK," she whispered, touching my hair.

"Because even if you think it's stupid to want that, I just, I want, I don't want to think about my career. I'm twelve —"

"I know," she interrupted, but I jumped right back in.

"It's hard because, I love when you look at me like I'm special." Her eyes were steady on mine. I didn't look away. "And you do everything for me," I said. "You give me so much. I know I have a gift and opportunities, and I want you to be proud, and, God, I don't want you to stop looking at me." I took a breath and stared down at my dirty sneakers. "But also I want to, to lose a three-legged race. I know that's ridiculous but I just, that's what I want."

A car passed outside, its tires sticky-sounding on the pavement. I raised my eyes to my window and focused on the streetlight, letting my vision blur.

Mom touched my forehead, lightly, and slowly brushed the hair back with her palm. "OK," she said.

"Thank you," I whispered, without taking my eyes off the light outside.

She pulled her arm back and rested her head on her knees, mirroring me. "You know," she said, "you don't have to be exactly like me for me to love you. But you do have to let me know who you are, and whoever that is, I'll love."

But not be proud of, I thought, looking at her. I didn't want her to have to lie, though, so instead of making her promise to be proud of me, I just asked, "Promise?"

"I'll always love you, no matter what." She reached across my knees to hug me. It didn't quite work. We were both off-balance and cramped, so we ended the hug quickly and smiled little grins at each other.

I pulled off my sneakers, for something to do, and said, "Thanks."

"Don't ever worry about that," she said, spinning my dinner plate a quarter turn.

We were both trying to pretend everything was all patched up, I could tell, and though I had been sitting here promising myself no more lies, I still didn't have the courage or the words to be honest about everything still not feeling OK. "OK," I said. We both smiled again without showing any teeth and let out deep breaths.

She bit her lip but didn't look up at me. "I just wish we'd been able to discuss this before."

"I'm sorry," I said, straightening my legs.

"Paul was sure you had run away."

"Really?" We looked at each other.

"He felt he'd hurt you by saying he wanted Zoe to be his sister. He was sure it was all his fault."

"Oh, Paul." I sighed.

Mom shrugged. "None of us knew what to think. It's just so unlike you to do anything like this."

"Daddy hates me."

"No," Mom said. "He loves you. But it's going to take him some time to finish being angry about this."

"I'm sorry," I said again. "You should punish me."

"The point isn't punishment, CJ." She stood up. I watched her perfectly white Keds step gracefully across my floor, over my dirty ones, half a size smaller. It had started to drizzle, which I hadn't noticed. She slammed my window closed. "The school is going to punish you, anyway, to make an example of you. Mrs. Johnson said you're going to have in-school suspension for the rest of the week." Mom leaned against my wall, crossing her arms over her chest. Lightning crackled in the sky behind her.

"Really?" I asked.

She nodded as thunder boomed. "I'm not sure what that is, actually."

"Everybody will stare at me all day," I explained. "You have to sweep the auditorium and Windex the front doors and, in between, sit in a chair outside Mrs. Johnson's office, doing nothing."

"Ooo," Mom said. She slid down to the floor, bumping into my dinner plate. "Well, but you know what? I'm not going to intercede with Mrs. Johnson. I'm not going to ask her to go easy on you."

"Good," I said, moving the plate out of her way. "You shouldn't. I guess. All week?"

Mom stood up and straightened her slacks. "That's what she told us."

I nodded. "Mom?"

"Mmm-hmm?"

"I really am sorry."

"Me, too, CJ," Mom said, standing up again. "Me, too."

She left without kissing me. I sat in the corner for a long time, watching the rain.

twenty-three

I have a very complex relationship with Tchaikovsky. Also with my mother.

I sat on the bench, banging my new cleats against the firm-packed dirt and imagining myself dancing the final adagio from Tchaikovsky's *Swan Lake.* As I died long-necked and alone in the spotlight, Coach Cress called my name. I looked up slowly. She sent me out onto the brown field, where I ran around in circles far from the soccer ball for the final three minutes until the ref's whistle blew and I found myself in the crush of purple jerseys that meant we had won. Through the bodies of my friends, I looked to the sidelines where my mother sat solemnly among the other chattering mothers. I turned away and followed my best friend, who'd scored two goals off the girls whose fingers we now brushed as we mumbled, "Good game."

After, at the pizza place, my teammates grabbed slices steaming hot off the tins and recounted the game, nodding, chewing. My mother had gone home, as I'd asked her to. I knew she was sitting straight-backed on her cow-stenciled stool, working up a smile for the daughter who had chosen to slump in clean cleats on a middle school soccer bench instead of to dance in the spotlight. As I pictured her, the *Swan Lake* music in my head drowned out my friends' voices.

THE FRIENDSHIP RING

CHECK OUT THIS SNEAK PREVIEW FROM

not that i care

After school, my best friend, CJ Hurley, got asked out. She called me right away to tell me, of course, but I was out riding my bike around. Friday had been a stressful day, socially. CJ left me a message on the machine — "Hello, this is a message for Morgan — Morgan? Tommy Levit just asked me out. Call me." All weekend I kept meaning to call her back, but I didn't get the chance. Not that I wasn't happy for her. I don't like Tommy anymore.

I just really got into this project, searching for ten perfect things. I barely talked to anybody. "Bring Yourself in a Sack?" my brother asked. "I remember that project." But I didn't want his help.

I was in a great mood when I got to school this morning, with my Sack full of ten complicated, meaningful symbols. The janitor was just unlocking the front doors, I got to school so early. I slid my bike into the rack and waited on the wall for CJ.

When her mother dropped her off, CJ ran over and climbed up onto the wall beside me. She didn't say anything about my not calling her back; she knows I'm really bad about that and she's used to it. Or I thought so, anyway. We talked about Tommy. I told her not to worry that they didn't talk all weekend, after the asking out; when I went out with him last year he never called me, either. Then we talked about whether Tommy's twin brother Jonas would ask me out today, like he was supposed to, and how fun it would be if the four of us were a foursome, and whether or not Jonas's curly hair is goofy. CJ used to like Jonas but now she's going out with Tommy, which is fine with me.

Not that she cares.

I guess actually, now that I think about it, I was doing all the chatting. CJ wasn't saying anything about becoming a foursome. She was just sitting there all pale, her deep-set green eyes looking anywhere but at me, her tight skinny body even tauter than usual. I didn't notice she was acting weird until too late.

Anyway.

Mrs. Shepard is walking toward the front of the class. I hold my breath while she passes me. When my brother Ned was in seventh grade, four years go, he said Mrs. Shepard was "real" because she wouldn't paste stars on every pretentious, childish poem full of clichés. I took my poem off the refrigerator. I vowed I'd make Mrs.

Shepard like me when I got to seventh grade. So far she doesn't particularly, but it's only the third week of school. I still have a shot.

I'm lying low in my seat now, clutching the bag and squeezing my eyes shut as Mrs. Shepard speaks. "I want to hear a clear, concise explanation of each item, why you chose it, and what about your character the item symbolizes."

We have to explain? I would've chosen all different things.

I don't know what I was thinking would happen with this Sack. Definitely NOT that I would have to unload my life from this brown paper bag like spreading my lunch on the cafeteria table for everybody to inspect and judge. No, no. Thanks anyway.

"Are there any questions?" Mrs. Shepard asks.

Right. Nobody raises a hand with a question, of course. I can't look around to see if everybody else seems relaxed and ready, if it's just me who's hiding under a desk.

"Good," Mrs. Shepard says, turning her helmet-head to look at each of us. Her white-blond hair is pasted into a hairdo, the kind that never moves, the kind that only gets washed once a week, at the beauty parlor. She reminds me of an owl, with her round piercing eyes and small hooked nose. Maybe it's the way she rotates her big head that's plunked deep between her shoulders. I did a report last year on owls. They're birds of prey. I sink down lower, imagining myself a field mouse trying to camouflage with the fake wood and putty-colored metal of my desk.

Please don't call on me.

"Olivia Pogostin," Mrs. Shepard calls.

Olivia Pogostin is my new best friend, as of today. I whispered with her all through lunch which was a little awkward for both of us, but we managed. She was actually sort of witty, and she gets the pretzel sticks that come in an individually wrapped box in her lunch, definitely a plus. My mother would never waste the money on those. We buy economy size everything, then take how much we need. We have one type of cookies for weeks at a time, until we finish and go back to Price Club. If there's a big sale, she might let us get a sleeve of individual potato chip bags. I always feel good if I open my lunch and there's a small sealed bag of chips in there. It looks so appropriate. CJ just gets a yogurt, every day, a yogurt and that's it. Not that they can't afford more. She just has to worry, because of ballet.

I sort of liked Olivia, today at lunch. Not as deadly wonkish as I had always figured. She had some funny things to say about girls like CJ who forget their friends as soon as a boy calls her on the phone. And, of course, there's the pretzels.

Olivia walks up to the front of the class. Her coarse black pigtails don't bounce, just jut adamantly out to the sides. She's the smallest person in seventh grade by a lot, and also the smartest if you don't count Ken Carpenter.

Olivia places her brown paper bag on Mrs. Shepard's desk, turns to face the class, and says, in her calm, steady monotone, "So. This is me."

What am I going to do? I can't present my items. My

palms are starting to sweat on the brown paper of my Sack. This is me? No way I would ever get up and say "This is me." Especially with this unexplainable stuff to explain.

Olivia pulls a charcoal pencil out of her paper bag, holds it up in front of her serious, calm face and annouces, "Charcoal pencils because I like to draw." She places it on Mrs. Shepard's desk blotter. Mrs. Shepard is nodding, over by the door. Teachers love Olivia; she does everything right. I didn't know it was supposed to be, like, hobbies.

"A calculator," Olivia says, lifting it. Her eyes focus above our heads on the back wall. "Because math is my favorite subject." She sets it down.

I catch myself twirling the bottom of my black polo

shirt and force myself to stop. My eyes, betraying me, glance over to my left. Next to me, CJ is sitting straight as a two-by-four on the edge of her chair, her head balanced gracefully on her long neck.

Olivia reaches into her Sack and pulls out a small box. I clamp my jaw shut and count. Sit up straight. My posture is good, too.

Olivia pulls a pair of earrings out of the box. I can't stop blinking.

"These are soccer ball earrings which represent me both because soccer is my favorite sport and also because I just got my ears pierced this summer."

Olivia glances at Mrs. Shepard, who hasn't budged. Ned told me that one time Mrs. Shepard told him, "Well said," and the whole class practically fainted.

Olivia swallows hard. Poor Olivia. I wonder what she's thinking. I don't know her that well, yet, but I'm sure she's off balance, not having the teacher nodding at her for once. If she looks at me, I decide, I'll smile encouragingly. It must be hard, sort of, to expect praise all the time. Not that I'd know; I'm just guessing.

I prepare to be supportive. Olivia doesn't look at me. Which is fine. Whatever. She doesn't look at anybody else either, at least. Staring at the back wall, she pulls a thick paperback book out of her bag. "A dictionary because I'm interested in etymology," she says.

I have no idea what that means. Nothing in my bag can be explained in a sentence. I did the whole thing wrong. What am I going to do?

"A pool ball because I like to shoot pool."

Oh, shut up already Olivia, I almost say out loud. I open my crumpled brown bag just enough to peek inside. Wrong, wrong, wrong; no pool balls, no charcoal pencils. I have a broken thermometer. A Barbie head. A twig. Nothing I could possibly explain to these nineteen other seventh graders who've known me my whole life but have no clue. Not even to CJ, who was my best friend from the beginning of fourth grade until today.

I'm twirling the bottom of my shirt with my finger again. It shames me if my clothes are wrinkled, it looks like I'm poor. Stop it. Pay attention to Olivia. My best friend. I blow the long bangs out of my eyes. They drive me crazy but at least they hide the pimples on my forehead, four of them and a fresh one coming. Don't touch, the oil from fingers makes it worse. Think, think — what am I going to do? The back of my thighs are sticking to the chair. Olivia is finishing, thank the lord. I don't know if we're supposed to clap or what. I'm not going to be the first one. I wedge my hands under my thighs and blow at my bangs again.

I don't know what I was thinking. It's not like I'm so close with Mrs. Shepard I want her to be in on all my private business; in fact, I don't really like her at all, the owl. I just got so involved, all weekend, choosing my ten items, I didn't think of how they'd be presented. I guess I thought we'd just hand our Sacks in.

Olivia is heading back to her seat, the desk in front of mine. I make the mistake of glancing toward CJ again. She looks at me with a big sad apology all over her face.

Save it, pal. It's not like I care or anything. I'm just trying to get through the day and please, you are totally free to do whatever you want. It makes no difference, I've dealt with more than you'll ever know, you pampered little prima donna. It would take a lot more than you to hurt me.

ABOUT THE AUTHOR

RACHEL VAIL has written four other well-received novels for adolescents, including, WONDER, an *American Bookseller* "Pick of the Lists," which Judy Blume called "Wonderful!"; DARING TO BE ABIGAIL, a *School Library Journal* Best Book of the Year; DO-OVER, a Recommended Book for Reluctant Young Readers; and EVER AFTER, which was one of the New York Public Library's 100 Best Children's Books in 1994.

She lives with her husband and young son in New York City.